I0659431

Aliens

The truth is the Tititri have been here longer than any of us suspected. They have already established an outpost on earth.

Family

His sister clutched his arm and whispered, "We have to treat her as if she is normal."

"What's normal? The aliens, the Tititri?"

The Mission

"We've got a schedule to meet. I need your commitment now. Otherwise I will get somebody else for the mission."

Of course Landon wanted to go, but something held him back. His daughter, Molly, and the Tititri.

Rebecca S. W. Bates

Can Thrill You Quickly

With These Short Story Collections

The Time is Light: The relationship between time and light in the cosmos.

Sharing Sol: The challenges of space exploration when somebody else is also out there.

Tough Mothers: Being a mother in space leads to all sorts of complications.

Available in e-books format for all e-readers.

Prelude to Proxima

Rebecca S. W. Bates

D. M. Kreg Publishing

DMKregPublishing.com

Copyright © 2015 by D.M. Kreg Publishing and
Rebecca S. W. Bates.

All rights reserved, including the right of reproduction, in whole
or in part in any form. This book is a work of fiction. Names,
characters, places and incidents either are products of the author's imagination or are used fictitiously. Any resemblance to
actual events or locales or persons, living or dead, is entirely
coincidental.

Cover Design: Renee Barratt, The Cover Counts

In loving memory of Aunt Esther, who made me believe that all dreams are possible.

Acknowledgments

Thanks to the many writers who helped with this project, including the Inklings and the Oregon Writers Network. This mission to Centauri couldn't go without their keen insights and awesome support. Special thanks to my family for enduring disruptions to our vacations and believing in me. Thanks also to Donald Kreg, editor and publisher extraordinaire.

Prelude to Proxima

Rebecca S. W. Bates

CHAPTER ONE

THE HOLOGRAPHIC IMAGE OF A dead man sprang to life before Landon Walker.

Goosebumps prickled the back of his neck in spite of the steamy air. His forearm stuck to the gummy surface of his desktop as he adjusted the house controls. The automatic climate system thrummed and squealed, working at capacity to thin the air of his private suite here at the International Space Agency's headquarters in Goiás, Brazil, but to little avail.

H.F. Washington, Landon's dead mentor and former boss, paced in full, life size in the display pit of this suite's personal holographic system. The illusion made H.F. appear as if he stood only an arm's reach away from Landon, but in reality, his boss had been dead more than a month. Already it was April, 2092, and the mission to track down the alien signal to Proxima Centauri would be delayed yet again, at least another two weeks. Landon was 51, not so old as the twenty-first century waned, but he felt his aging. The mission couldn't afford to waste more time.

"In the event of my untimely death," the holo image of H.F. said, "you must carry on, my boy."

Landon crouched forward, creaking the vinyl on the edge of

his chair. That old tag used to annoy him when H.F. was alive. Now it only reminded him how much he missed the old man. It also told him that this message was clearly meant for *him*. When had H.F. recorded it, anyway? He hadn't found it before now because somehow the old-fashioned stick containing the data had ended up in a pocket inside his travel bag. H.F. must've put it there, guessing that it wouldn't be found until he packed for an overnight trip. With such precaution, H.F. must've worried more about terrorism than he'd let on. The persons responsible for the bomb last month hadn't been caught yet, but Landon felt certain they were the terrorists known as Savers. The bomb had probably been meant for the spaceplane, but it ended up killing H.F.

His holo mane of gray hair flapped wildly about him as he strode back and forth, aimlessly fingering his trademark worry beads. "The Tititri won't stop with my death," he said.

An electric charge raced through Landon at the mention of the aliens' name. The memory of the night before lingered fresh in his mind, when an alien entity spoke to him through his two-year-old daughter, Molly. It was over now, he told himself. His daughter was safe, as safe as she could be with his sister Greer. The aliens, gone.

H.F. continued, his voice rumbling out of the four-foot square holo pit. "The Tititri won't stop until they've taken all of Earth. Their signal... The destruction at Valles Marineris... What we thought was only the beginning... It wasn't. You were right, my boy, when you suspected that I wasn't being entirely forthright with you. I'm sorry. I thought if you knew any more about this matter back then... Well, I didn't know what you might've done. I was afraid we could never persuade you to join our team. You haven't exactly kept an open mind on this subject. Despite the evidence. But if you've found this message, then it's because you're ready to hear the truth. And the truth is, the Tititri have been here longer than any of us ever suspected. It only came to my attention about a year ago, around the time of your difficulties with your wife. You see, the Tititri have already established an outpost here on Earth, for the purpose of receiving the signal from their home planet."

Landon sprang up from his desk, knocking the chair over backwards. His sudden movement tore a new wave of pain to his shoulder, wounded by a grazing bullet the night before. How could H.F. possibly have known the aliens had an outpost here on Earth? And if so, then where was it?

The holo H.F. paused his monologue and chuckled, as if anticipating Landon's reaction. The old man knew him better than anyone. He had been like a father to Landon. "It's in Patagonia," he said, lowering his voice. "Where Summer is."

Landon sucked in his breath. He was flying to Patagonia today to try one last time to get through to Summer, his ex-wife. He couldn't begin to consider an offer that would require him to leave on a mission for twenty-four years, not before he found closure to a relationship that had ended badly. Now H.F.'s message suggested that Summer's presence there had something to do with the *aliens*. Maybe the aliens' business with Molly the night before had nothing at all to do with him. They'd targeted Molly because she was Summer's daughter.

"The signal," H.F. said, "was meant to arrive when the time was right to awaken the Tititri from their dormancy and begin their invasion."

Landon swiped one hand across his buzz cut. H.F. was

talking about the tachyonic emission that Landon's lab on SpaceHab had intercepted with his collector. Other labs hadn't been able to duplicate his work yet.

But it could be done. He had collected tachyons. Collecting those faster-than-light particles for the purpose of instantaneous communication was his work, his life.

H.F.'s image paced out of range of the holo field and then back again. "Now do you see my urgency? Why we so desperately need to colonize new worlds? I couldn't tell you before about the dormant aliens because of your...shall we say your *sensitivity* to the subject. On account of Summer. It's not a coincidence, my boy, that she happens to be in Patagonia Prison. You see, the aliens arranged it for her. They chose her to be the guardian of their outpost. You must persuade her to help us stop the alien invasion."

A chill coursed down Landon's spine as the image fizzled away, dissolving on a puff of air. Where had H.F. gotten his information? If what he said was true — and he'd never known the old man to be wrong — then the aliens had been in contact with Summer all along. That might explain her strange behavior, but...

He struggled to understand.

His break-up with Summer and her arrest had happened too fast. He thought he was going to Patagonia to understand the reasons behind her betrayal, why she'd tried to kill them all. And why she'd arranged her pregnancy despite their agreement to postpone children indefinitely. Molly was born without Landon's knowledge, while he'd been away on another mission, the one to Titan. He'd thought the Savers had brainwashed her into joining their terrorist cause, which ultimately led to her failed attempt to bomb SpaceHab. It had landed her in Patagonia Prison.

H.F. was suggesting that Summer's actions had been master-minded instead by *aliens*.

Landon sighed and flipped off his data control. His old boss, H.F. Washington, the man most responsible for sending humanity to space once again, whose remains awaited in cryo-storage for possible reconstruction one day, had always loved drama. Now, in the absence of his holo image, the room felt empty. Cold, with a muggy chill.

Landon righted his chair and yanked out the data stick. The sudden twisting movement brought a flare of renewed pain to his shoulder, like needles digging into a raw wound. It had only been a flesh wound, for pity's sake. That deranged reporter's bullet from an antique gun had only nicked his shoulder the night before. He'd been lucky.

He dropped the stick back into his travel bag and snapped it shut. The cart would arrive soon with Molly and Greer. He checked the time on his personal valet. His sister was late.

He couldn't stop thinking about the events that played out in the pocket of jungle the night before, rescuing Molly from her kidnappers, getting shot in the process. Those events had led to the last-minute offer that Landon fill one of the empty seats on the Centauri mission.

He needed a few days to make his decision, he'd told Sam, who'd replaced H.F. as the new boss at ISA, but he already knew what he was going to have to do. He couldn't possibly abandon Molly. So he would have to decline the offer. It would've been his scientist's dream to be included on such a mission. He hadn't turned it down yet because he held out hope that he could find a way to make it work. Perhaps he would find his answers along with his closure with Summer.

Invasion, H.F. had said. Landon hoped the word choice was only another example of the old man's keen taste for drama, but if not... Could Earth survive whatever the aliens — the Tititri — had in mind for them?

CHAPTER TWO

ZIZA FONSECA ITCHED ALL OVER. Bug bites covered her exposed flesh. Bugs zzzzz-ed around her face. Bugs crawled under her pants, soaked from jungle damp and stinking with the poison of city sweat.

Ziza itched from the inside out.

Parrots screeched at her, yelling at her that she was an unwelcome parasite plunging through their wetly green world. She slapped her way through the never-ending wall of dripping fronds, weaving and ducking. Bobbing leaves splattered her with the rotting smells of who knew what, rotting beneath layers of death, piling up since before Mãe's time.

Cobwebs plastered to Ziza's face and pushed their dusty taste of spiders down her throat as she pressed on. There was no escape. She could never flee her jungle origins. She had been wrong ever to think it possible. She had been wrong to believe the recruiters who had once upon a time told her about the re-education camps down south. Lies, all. Once born into the jungle, you could never escape it.

Beneath the ringing, hissing, clicking, sawing, slurping sounds of the jungle pulsed another sound. One that did not belong. Something thumped behind her. Too heavy for a panther's paws. Too agile for a tapir.

She paused, choking for breath in the damp, muggy air that was almost too thick to breathe. The thumping pulse that she had heard behind her must have paused too. All she could hear — besides the rings, the hisses, the clicks, the saws, the slurps — was the hammering of her heart, echoing in her head. Had she imagined something else?

No. She was just a ball of nerves. And no wonder, after the disaster of the night before. That was it. The memory of last night was all that rang in her head. Nothing more.

The night had ended badly, on account of the gun. She had followed the bidding of the Mundomba, taking the little girl back to Ziza's people. But the introduction of the gun last night changed everything. The dance their great leader wished them to dance, the dance of the moon, their protector, could not be danced. Her people had scattered into the jungle, because of the gun, and so had she.

They'd all fled, giving up all hopes for their new lives of peace under the moon.

Morning had come and gone, and Ziza was still running. She was forever running from her old life, but getting nowhere. Until she made a new plan, she would keep on running, not knowing where to run to. Or her purpose.

"What do we do now?" she asked the parasite that lodged within her.

She did not know what the thing was that rode inside her, only that Mãe had put it there. Why not? Mãe, her mother, but also a high priestess of the Mundomba cult, had used her magic with the moonrose vine to infect Ziza with the parasite. And then Mãe died. Ever since, the parasite usually tingled, making

Ziza's arms and legs move in ways that Ziza did not plan. It was probably a thing like Mãe's spirit. Today it felt like a dead weight.

"Now what do we do?"

But no answer tickled her mind, nothing more than an itch she could not scratch, and so she kept running. Only parrots screeched at her as she ran through Mãe's jungle. Always running.

She'd vowed never to return here, and now here she was, worse off than before, when she'd left it the first time. Lost in the jungle. Separated from her people. From any people. With no way to get back home. And someone — or some*thing* — on her tail.

Ziza felt all run out. She collapsed in a heap on the muddy bank of a stream. Monkeys howled at her as she wept.

CHAPTER THREE

THE MOON GLOWED FROM BEHIND a thin band of clouds and touched the river with a streak of rippling light, a silvery arrow oozing, flooding into the dark of the jungle, showing him the way. Even in his dream, water slapped him as he plunged forward. Mosquitoes buzzed his ears. Chants pulsed the thick night air.

Tee-tee-tree...

A sting to his shoulder, and he was rolling, tumbling... Dizzy... Warm wetness trickled down his arm. Blood. Something whirred inside his head. Something important he had to do.

Tee-tee-tree...

Somehow he staggered to his feet and plunged on, tripping to the water's edge, the edge of a swamp that surrounded a flooded village. Swamp currents slid in and around, searching for a way inside the crumbling plaster huts.

One pink porch displayed a row of columns, holding up its thatched roof, and then the columns shifted, and they weren't columns any longer but women. Writhing, naked women uplifted their bronze arms, glistening with sweat. A tunnel of their arms led toward a central figure, the priestess, also naked except for the garland of fish skulls she wore round her throat.

Tee-tee-tree...

A girl child — his Molly! — drifted through the tunnel of arms. She danced and twirled before the priestess, whose ample layers of flesh shuddered and rippled. Her eyes rolled back into her head, leaving only the whites exposed in a face, more black than night.

Teee-teee-treee... *It was Molly singing.*

The chorus of naked women sloshed through floodwaters, creeping, crawling closer to Molly. Their eyes glowed with fever. Their lips parted hungrily.

A green light flickered from within Molly's eyes, as green as an underwater garden. A woman's face shone from under the child's face.

We told you not to come, *a woman's husky voice said-sang from within Molly's child's body.*

* * * * *

Landon jolted awake, his heart racing. His breath came in choking gasps as the dream evaporated from his memory.

Form-fitting cushions of a seat embraced him. *Not* the flooded river of the jungle. He'd escaped. With Molly and Greer. The night before.

Now he was *here*, aboard the International Space Agency's private twelve-seater. A cushy seat tilted him back into its bean pod configuration. Leather smells piped into the cabin air with an impression of wealth. He'd given in to sleep while the shearjet zipped south at supersonic speeds. All he heard through the earplugs was a steady thrum of the engines whispering in his ears.

Prelude to Proxima

Two-year-old Molly sat on the floor at the front of the plane, acting oblivious to the presence of her father and aunt. She stacked blocks into towers, and then in a frenzy of whirling arms, crashed them apart. Her throaty giggle as she destroyed her towers sounded almost demonic, sending chills down Landon's spine. It wasn't an innocent gurgle or squeal. In fact, he'd never heard baby talk from her. The only sounds she made were something much deeper, much more ancient.

His feet pressed against the footrest, flipping his seat into an upright position. He plucked the plugs from his ears and leaned across the aisle toward his sister. The three of them were the only passengers. "I'm going to strap her into her pod."

"Let her play, Landie. We're not there yet."

He unbuckled himself and rose, flinching with a brief stab of pain. The wound under the bandage under his dress shirt was still new. As a martial artist, he would have to toughen up, train his brain to ignore the message. He would need all the strength he could muster if he was going to resist the aliens who wanted his daughter.

Greer clutched his arm and whispered. "We have to treat her as if she's normal."

"What's normal?" Until recently, he thought he had known. Now, he wasn't sure about anything, except that he didn't like the way Molly sat so exposed, playing out there in the open. Her energy radiated her whereabouts to anyone who might be looking for her.

Such as, the aliens. The Tititri.

They were gone now, but they would come back. He was sure of it, even though he didn't know the Tititri's capabilities. He didn't know what he was fighting against. If H.F. was right, then Landon was bringing his daughter to the land of the aliens' outpost. Within closer reach of the aliens. He didn't know how they'd accessed her before, but he suspected they'd done it through her tracking chip, the chip that had enabled him to find her in the jungle the night before. He hoped the pod's shield would buffer her now from any probes.

"Careful, Landie, don't touch her bug bites. Poor baby is coated with them."

He didn't see any welts. Nothing marred the baby flesh of her arms and legs, neck and face. His sister always exaggerated. He scooped up Molly despite her yelps of protest and the hot knife sensation searing his shoulder.

"I did my best to soothe her with creams," Greer said. "We were nearly eaten alive out there in the jungle last night. I thought we were all going to die."

"Bugs were the least of our problems," he said, carrying Molly to her seat pod. He strapped her in and palmed the latch. A clear shield irised out from the sides of the pod and slid into the shape of a bubble around her. Through its transparency, he could see a strand of her strawberry blonde hair flutter as air currents circulated inside her pod. The shield muted the child's whines.

"You can stop worrying about the aliens," Greer said. "If they wanted to hurt us, they would've done so by now. On the other hand, those people in the jungle last night were a whole lot more dangerous."

"We might be able to control the damage. That is, as long as you keep quiet about the aliens."

"*Me?*"

"You can't talk about them, Greer. Not one word, not to

anyone. It's important. Last night was a perfect example of how the rest of the world would react if word leaked out about any alien presence."

"Well then, why are you talking about it? Molilia will hear you."

"She can't hear us through the shield. And I want you to call her 'Molly'. Not that lame name Summer came up with."

She sighed. "But Landie, it's a beautiful name."

"And that's another thing," he said with a scowl. "I'm Landon." His critics had called him far worse than the nickname his ex-wife had given him and Greer had adopted. He didn't need his own sister to remind him of Summer. His failures with his ex-wife haunted him enough. But then, she'd failed *him*, too.

Greer climbed out of her seat with a huff and headed to Molly's pod. She reached for the touchpad that would release the shield.

"Don't," Landon said. Now his head throbbed as well as his shoulder. "It's for her own safety."

"What are you worried about? She's safe. She's wearing her *figa*, after all."

"That's just a good luck charm."

"It worked last night, didn't it? Otherwise, we wouldn't have gotten away from those drugged-up cult women."

"We got lucky," he said, but Greer was right. He had used the sign of the *figa*, a human hand with the thumb tucked between the index and middle fingers, and his action seemed to surprise the cult women — the Mundomba. That surprise had allowed him to escape with Molly and Greer.

Greer rummaged through one of her bags and pulled out

a stuffed toy, a parrot that Molly had mashed with her love. "She's all alone in there. I'm just going to give her something to hug." She offered it to Molly, then sealed the shield back into place and returned to her seat.

"What's with you, anyway?" Greer said. "Are you just feeling touchy because Sam Talcott is in charge now?"

"Don't play psychologist with me, Greer." He closed his eyes, hoping she would get the hint that he wanted to go back to sleep.

She didn't.

"He's up to something," she said. "You know what it is, don't you?"

He sighed. "I don't know anything."

"He's the one who arranged for that jungle woman to baby-sit Molil— I mean, Molly." She huffed. "Have it your way. I thought I could trust Sam to find someone reliable, or at least someone who wasn't going to end up kidnapping the baby, f'goodness sake."

"The Tititri did it, not Sam. The woman was just the courier."

"But they're all in it together, aren't they? And because of them, because of whatever it is that they're up to, you're dragging all of us off to Patagonia today."

"I have to see Summer one last time."

"I don't think that's such a good idea. Molil— Molly shouldn't see her mother in her terrible conditions. Besides, what do you mean 'one last time'? You're not going on the mission."

He said nothing, and she went on. "You can't go to Proxima Centauri, so don't even think it. You *can't*. What about us? What about your family?"

"Stop worrying. Sam hasn't made any changes to the roster yet." To be more precise, Landon hadn't figured out yet how to negotiate Sam's offer into a deal they could all live with.

"I wouldn't trust any changes he tries to make." Greer wouldn't shut up. "What do you know about him, anyway?"

"Not much. Sam Talcott has none of the clout that H.F. had." With the death of H.F., now Sam was in charge of the old man's dreams.

"Well, clearly he has *some* clout, since he managed to pull together this trip to Patagonia so fast."

"Because it's important." He bit his tongue to keep from slipping it out, because Greer couldn't keep a secret if her life depended on it. *H.F. thought the aliens had an outpost in Patagonia.*

"A-ha. So this little side trip to Patagonia has something to do with the mission to Proxima Centauri?"

He ignored her question and turned to watch his daughter inside the bubble shield. Molly bent earnestly over her stuffed parrot, the same way he'd seen Summer lean over her as a baby. He wondered when things had gone wrong with Summer.

Greer rattled on, interrupting his reverie. "Don't tell me there's something between Sam and Summer."

Landon grunted and reached for his cup of iced tea to douse the flames of his irritation from Greer's suggestion.

"Pay attention, silly," she said, slapping his hand. "How long have you known Sam?"

The aisle separating them wasn't wide enough to keep her from invading his personal space. "Not much longer than you. I only first met him when H.F. brought him on board at ISA last August. Eight months ago."

She sighed the long and drawn-out sound of exasperation indicating her opinion that he was a dimwit. "But you've known *of* him much longer, right?"

"Sure. Who hasn't? He's the famous astronaut who flew the Jupiter missions with Masambwa."

"Something happened out there, didn't it? He said something to me about it, but it didn't make sense. And you were talking about it too, or rather, I should say *arguing* about it at dinner the other night. The night before..." Her voice drifted to a whisper as she blinked and nodded her head at Molly. "... they kidnapped Molil— Molly."

"Listen, Greer. Don't say a word about the aliens. I mean it. This may be more important than you can understand right now."

His mind still spun in the aftermath of the events the day before. He wondered if the standard children's chip embedded at the base of Molly's head had enabled the aliens, the Tititri, to access her.

"Well?" Greer said, reaching across the aisle to poke him again.

He blotted up the tea spills with his napkin. Where was that steward bot when he needed its assistance? "Well what?"

"Aren't you going to tell me why it's so important? Aren't you going to tell me why you think I'm so stupid that I couldn't possibly understand? I'll bet whatever it is, *that's* what's wrong with Sam. Just so you know. Whatever happened on Jupiter is what screwed him up."

He fought a smile but said nothing, not wanting to encourage Greer.

"Pay attention," she said with another jab to his forearm.

28

"Is *that* what this is all about?"

"You'll find out soon enough."

"Stop it. Just stop it. I can take the hint. You don't want to talk about it. Fine." Pushing out of her seat, she flounced up the aisle to an entertainment cabinet.

Greer didn't know yet that he intended to fight for her to go on the mission, too. It would be the only way he could make his deal work. He couldn't take Molly without her because technically, she was Molly's guardian. The Worlds Court had handed his daughter over to Greer when they decreed Landon's failure at parenting. All because he'd had Molly inserted into cryo-sleep.

Sure, it wasn't the best choice, but it hadn't hurt her. Cryo-sleep was perfectly safe these days. Besides, he hadn't been thinking straight. Summer had just been carted away. He'd needed to buy time, to find a better option for childcare while he worked, uninterrupted. The Worlds Court hadn't seen it that way.

In retrospect, maybe it was a mistake. Now Greer had been elevated to a more important position in his life, and he was stuck with it. His sister would probably consider a twenty-four-year detour to Proxima Centauri as the sort of interruption to her routine that she would refuse to accept.

Landon would have to convince her to go. Not only to help him care for Molly but also to protect his daughter from his own idiocy.

Okay, he admitted it.

Sometimes he was an idiot.

Greer was right. It had been his fault the chain of reaction had come down to this, and now he had to make things right.

Questions. So many questions.

He closed his eyes and wondered. *Aliens!* Landon had seen the alien ruins on Titan with his very own eyes, and up until then, he wouldn't have believed any of this. Maybe Titan was where it all started.

A new thrum vibrated the seat cushions and tickled Landon with its current, drawing him out of his memories and alerting him to glance out the porthole. The lumpy white blanket below resolved into snowy mountain peaks as the shearjet dropped out of its supersonic speed. They would be arriving soon at the private airstrip servicing the prison. Landon's chest tightened with apprehension.

It was unforgivable, what Summer had done, betraying him and everyone else. Or so he'd thought. It seemed that the Savers had recruited her into their terrorist group. They believed that Earth's use of technology would invite aliens to invade, and so they wanted to destroy technology, never mind that humans' radio signals had long since escaped Earth.

If H.F. was right, it wasn't Savers. It was aliens all along.

Savers... Aliens... Whoever was behind it, someone had brainwashed Summer into an attempt to blow up SpaceHab. That bomb failed to detonate, and she'd been hauled off to prison. The habitat in orbit remained safe, but Summer's bomb had succeeded at one thing: it had destroyed the trust that had been the foundation of their marriage.

And now... He didn't entirely understand why he felt so driven to settle up with her before making a decision to leave Earth for a quarter of a century. Was it possible he still...

No. Love was quite impossible anymore.

Why did it matter if he left Earth for that long without

seeing her again?

Molly.

Molly mattered beyond what he'd ever imagined possible. He'd been foolish not to want her. Look at her.

No longer controlled by aliens, she was a picture of innocence in a miniature version of Landon himself. She shared his facial features — his sharp jawline — only hers softened and glowed with curiosity instead of the way Landon always tightened his, hardened by the work that drove him. She shared his expressions of curiosity in the way she tilted her head to one side and furrowed her brow as if to see better inside the stuffed parrot, or whatever object she examined. He wondered if she knew about the alien that had spoken through her. She didn't talk, so she couldn't tell him what she did or did not know. Couldn't, or wouldn't?

The steward bot rolled out of a cabinet, activating the locking mechanisms that returned screens and tables to their receptacles. They were preparing to touch down, and it was time to pick up the blocks Molly had left strewn across the aisle. Greer, plugged into some entertainment filling her head, didn't appear concerned about Molly's things, so Landon rose from his pod, grimacing from the stab of pain to his shoulder. He gathered the blocks before the bot would reach them, having to plot a new course around the field of obstacles.

The blocks turned this way and that, some of them still standing in piles. Towers reminded him of the ruined ones on Titan.

He glanced over at her, almost fearing to see what his daughter had become. Now she seemed oblivious to Landon's concern. Her small body tensed, then jerked as she whipped

31

her head around to face the window.

Nothing but sky out there, baby girl.

Molly stared transfixed at the window. Her lips moved, touching each other, bouncing up and down, but no baby sounds babbled forth. Perhaps the shield blocked her sounds. It looked as if she was having a silent conversation with someone.

The bot rolled closer, securing and latching the loose items Greer had used and discarded during their flight down here from ISA headquarters.

Molly turned away from the window and studied the machine. Within her pod, she waved her arms, the same way she'd ripped apart her block towers. Her small hands thumped against the inside of her pod's shield. Suddenly the bot stopped its work. It looked frozen. As if it had malfunctioned.

Molly stared at the bot, her eyes glittering from hazel to glowing green.

Landon held his breath. Her eyes had changed to green the night before, when the alien spoke through her. He thought the alien was gone.

He was wrong.

CHAPTER FOUR

SUMMER JEUNNE-WALKER SHUFFLED up the side of the mountain, pushed onward, upward by the tilt of the guards' guns. Shackles pinched her ankles every time she stepped too far. Stupid shackles bound her to the ground, but they couldn't harness her mind.

Her mind soared free. She imagined what it would feel like to really soar up there in the crisp, mountain air currents. Free. Like the bird crying "*sque-e-e-e!*" somewhere above her head, an echo of her heart. She tilted her chin up a mere fraction, not so far up that the guard holding the gun would notice. Only far enough to roll her eyeballs upward. And see if...

If she could find the moon in this daytime sky.

It wasn't there, at least, not in the slice of sky she could see. It was a sky so intensely blue, the color seared her eyes and tears blurred her vision.

She felt alone without the moon, her healer. The moon had tried to soothe her, to fill her with its tranquility after the fuckup her life had become. Her single mission, a failure. The bomb hadn't blown. She should've been dead by now. Dead, like her baby was dead. But she hadn't died.

Not yet.

In her peripheral vision she saw the killing end of the guard's gun shake at her. He muttered words rapid-fire with a sharp edge that seemed to indicate both impatience and boredom. She couldn't hurry, though. The soles of her prison-issue boots were thick and rigid enough to protect her from the rocky sharpness of the uneven terrain, but the shackles kept her from stepping high enough to clear the jagged rocks without tripping. She could only manage tiny sliding steps, like a baby bird. Flightless.

She flared her nostrils. The prison doc had removed the poison filters and ear mics that had been surgically implanted when the Savers first recruited her. She felt vulnerable now without her implants. The doc and guards were just minions, servants to the officials of the Association of Worlds — she called them Asses — but they outraged her and fueled her contempt. For all of them. For this.

Imprisoned here, what chance did any of them have anymore? Against the alien invaders? The first wave of invasion would take the babies. The Tititri had already done that. Molilia had been the first. It was hopeless now. Humans were all dead. They just didn't know it yet.

Priiii!

Something hummed inside her head. Her spine stiffened, and she jerked around to find its origin. Another barrage of words fired back at her, rising in pitch, and the blunt end of a cold, metal stick jabbed against her shoulder blade. A second guard had come up behind her, shoving her with his gun.

She stumbled over a spear of rock, one of countless hundreds of protruding bits of granite, and fell. Her arms flung outward in a futile attempt to balance herself. The handcuffs worked against her, making her feel impossibly top-heavy. One knee cracked against a rock, her bound knuckles slammed against another rock, and her chin smacked into the hard-packed earth, busting her lip and giving her a mouthful of grit. Waves of searing pain crashed through her, numbing her, pressing her down to the bed-of-nails ground. Her teeth vibrated, her core spasmed, and her knee and knuckles felt like they were on fire. She yelped when she first went down, but she did not cry. She tightened her jaw and licked dirt and blood from her lower lip, stifling any cries that threatened to slip out.

That's what they wanted from her. Pitiful sobs. She would not give them what they wanted. Never. She was not pitiful. The moon knew. The gentle, serene moon.

Indecipherable words snarled between the guards. Chains rattled as the couple dozen men and women inmate workers heaved sighs and sank down onto boulders, taking a much-needed break from their climb up the side of the mountain to the dig site. Two other shackled and cuffed prisoners clanked over to Summer and positioned themselves one on either side of her. Their clouds of body odor enveloped her, blending with her own tang.

"Don't worry, we got you," said the one named Amazon, a giant block of a man. He nodded at the other one, Diamond, lean and sinewy as a steel cable.

Droplets of sweat creased trails through the filth and grime that caked their faces as they strained. Wedging her between them, they hauled Summer to her feet. Pain blazed through her, consuming her in its haze. Their compassion gave her the strength to stand, despite her busted knees.

Who knew their real names? Nothing real mattered

anymore. They were here in the suspended reality of Patagonia Prison for the same reason Summer was: eco-terrorism. That was the official charge. Murder, too, for them, but murder was the lesser charge. Summer hadn't actually murdered anyone, although she'd like to. Rumor had it that Amazon had personally killed many thousands in mass attacks at city centers around the world, while Diamond had confined himself to assassinating specific targets, master-minds of technology. Only a dozen or so of those assassinations could actually be pinned to him.

A nod of understanding passed between the three of them, bonding Summer to Amazon to Diamond. The Earth wars were coming. Not even all the Savers knew it yet — or maybe they did, maybe that's why they'd abandoned her — but actually, the wars had already started. Summer knew, on account of the baby. The Tititri had forced the baby on her, and then they'd taken it away. She and Amazon and Diamond might have to wait out the wars here in Patagonia, powerless to prevent how they played out, but the wars would go on, regardless. They'd made their own sacrifices long ago when they'd joined the Savers in the rebel cause against invading aliens.

And now they couldn't do a goddamned thing, except build a road to nowhere.

No! Save her! The humming sounded like a whispering voice near Summer's head.

She twisted around, searching for the speaker. It sounded as if someone had said "no Saver." Yes, she was a Saver, but no one was there who might have spoken.

It was a hum, but it had sounded like a voice, and it had come from *inside* her head. The way it had before coming to Patagonia, when the Savers had given her instructions through the microphones implanted in her inner ears. She thought the doc had removed them, too, when she'd arrived at the prison. Was she wrong? They were trying to confuse her.

Amazon and Diamond reacted with recognition flickering in their eyes, black and simmering as smoldering coal.

"Did you hear something?" she whispered.

Amazon frowned, creasing more sweat trails.

"It's not the same as what you hear," Diamond said with a grunt.

"How do you know what I hear?" Summer said.

"We all got different jobs," said Diamond.

The guards' voices interrupted, cutting the air with their staccato sounds. Summer thought one of them was going to throw her down to the ground again, the way he charged toward her. But Amazon stepped between them, and the guard stopped cold, jutting his chin close to Amazon's chest. The guard spat words at Amazon, but the giant prisoner simply gazed back, his jaw rippling with tension. Cords of twitching muscle joined the block of his head to his cement pillar-trunk. Muscle, instead of a neck. The guard glared at Summer, skimming his gaze the length of her body in the formless orange jumpsuit. He flicked an imaginary cigarette at her and then retreated to the boulder where two other guards hunkered.

"They're giving us half a minute to clean you up," Amazon said, using the coarse fabric of one of his sleeves to daub against her mouth. Cuffed together, his other arm dragged along with the daubing arm.

She felt her lip already puffing out, its flesh hanging limp. She turned her head away from his scraping motion and growled. "Enough. Why would they care if I bleed to death?"

"They don't," Diamond said. "They just don't want to lose one of their workers. That would slow them down too much, building their precious road. Can you walk?"

Summer leaned her weight on the leg with the bruised knee. Arrows of pain shot through her. "I'll get used to it. How do you know what I hear?"

"It's on your face when they talk to you. Everyone knows we still hear the Savers. Hell, even the guards know. That's why we're here in this shithole. The Asses want you to hear them. They want to trace the Savers through us." He snickered. "They keep it up, the guards are going to piss their pants. But you. You're special. How come the Savers want me and him to help you, like you was some sort of queen or something? What'd they tell you this time?"

"Not the Savers," Summer said. It was a different voice. Maybe not a voice at all. The sound had echoed a distant cry, reminding her of an elk's defiant bugle. She didn't think there were any elk here, but the mountain landscape recalled her heritage, haunting her with its sounds.

She shrugged it off and went on. "Anyway, you're wrong. The Savers don't talk to me anymore." Not since the disaster of her failed bomb attempt up on SpaceHab. Her rebel brothers and sisters had abandoned her in her time of greatest need.

"Well, they talk to someone," Amazon said. "Enemy's coming today. That's what I heard. That must be why the guards are in such a hurry for us to get their road done."

She shrugged, and the guards started shouting again.

"Break time is over," Diamond said. "Time to haul ass. We got our jobs to do." Diamond nodded at the flattened ridge ahead, the apparent destination of the switchbacking path they were widening into a road. Amazon nudged her from behind, gently supporting her, practically pushing her upwards.

What had the defiant voice meant? No Saver? Maybe she'd misunderstood. Again.

She'd tried to help the rebel cause once before, but she'd failed. That's why she'd ended up here. But maybe she hadn't failed. Maybe the intent all along was to bring her *here*. To position her here, where the Earth wars would start. This time she would have support, in the form of Amazon and Diamond. They were a team.

The trio trudged on up the hill, almost as a single unit within the line of prisoners. Pain fired each of Summer's limping steps, but she wouldn't give in to the throbbing waves. They made her dizzy, and she swayed with each new bird-step. Or maybe it was the altitude. They'd climbed nearly a thousand feet from the prison, which was already high enough up. She'd spent too many years at sea level, after having grown up in Colorado, and she'd lost her altitude adaptation, never mind she'd been here in the prison more than enough time to re-adapt. Nine weeks, or was it months? She'd lost track of the time. Nine something. Hell, maybe it was nine years.

She should've adapted by now, but she hadn't. Maybe she'd lost the piece of herself that would allow her to adapt. She was non-adaptable anymore.

She felt the guards' feverish anticipation as the inmates labored closer to the mountain pass. Guards urged them along with their guns. One of them carried a whip that he occasionally flicked to the ground beside their feet with a loud crack, dislodging loose rocks that tumbled and rolled against the sides of stumbling feet.

And then they crested the ridge with a loud, audible sigh rising up from the prisoners. The guards could wave their guns and whips all they wanted, but the prisoners stopped all the same, breathing deep, replenishing their lungs with as much oxygen as they could suck from the thin air. Summer felt faint. Humans were not meant to toil here.

The sound of tumbling waters drew her attention down into the valley far below. The river had cut this chasm eons ago, but today it was a landmark that riveted the attention of everyone, prisoners and guards alike. "There it is," someone murmured, nodding to one of the pieces of the river's silvery ribbon, twisting in and out around jumbles of boulders. With her eyes, she traced its course back to the glacier that remained, shrunken, in the shadowed cup of the mountainside.

There.

In its retreat, the edge of the glacier revealed three objects standing up like leafless tree trunks from the snow and ice. But they weren't trees. Not here, not above timberline. From here, half a mile away or so, the tips of the objects gleamed golden in the ebbing sun. They looked more like smoke stacks protruding from a buried city.

CHAPTER FIVE

THE SHEARJET SKIMMED THE summits of mountain peaks and then dropped suddenly, giving Landon the unnerving sensation of sinking. He felt as if his stomach pushed up his throat. But it wasn't really the descent that troubled him.

He'd seen the way his daughter had controlled the steward bot. Molly had kept the bot from completing its programmed circuit.

Why?

With the plane's sudden descent, the entire cabin angled as if it was sliding off the slope of a mountain. The same way his life was skidding off course from what it had been, his relatively comfortable world as a researcher — a misunderstood one, perhaps, but one who would contribute to H.F.'s dream of making long-distance space travel and colonization more likely, thanks to his tachyonic communication device.

If he hadn't seen his daughter's little demonstration, he would never have believed it. But then, who knew what the alien who'd targeted her was capable of doing?

The plane lurched, or maybe it was his stomach. He'd landed in worse situations. Probably his very worst gut-wrenching moment had been the shuttle drop to the surface of

Mars, where he'd done his post-doc many years ago. That time, the chutes failed to open until the last possible moment.

Patagonia was cake by comparison.

Notwithstanding the possible presence of an alien.

He'd seen Molly's eyes turn green when she did whatever she'd done to deactivate the steward bot. Which meant the alien had returned.

But maybe it had never left.

Shortly after the bot episode, Molly's eyes returned to their normal golden brown. Now, he couldn't be sure if that meant she was free of the alien, or if the alien had simply submerged somewhere deeper within her.

A voice — not Molly's — had sounded like a woman's and said clearly through Molly's mouth the night before, "we told you not to come." *We.* Meaning, there was more than one of them. Aliens.

H.F. had said in his holo message that the aliens were dormant, but clearly at least one of them had awakened.

We told you not to come. To Proxima? Or to that piece of jungle where the Mundomba women had kidnapped Molly? Maybe to Patagonia. Or else, what? They would make Molly deactivate the steward bot. A simple show of their power. What else could they do, he wondered.

Would they try to control *him*, through Molly?

He remembered the man who'd apparently hanged himself in the Holland Annex, Van Pelt, one of the few other researchers into tachyonic communication. Landon had met him a few times at colloquia, but he never knew him well, certainly not well enough to decipher the cryptic message he'd left behind in the form of a suicide note. Van Pelt had had some sort of encounter with the aliens. Maybe he'd killed himself to keep from being controlled by them. Or someone else had killed him to prevent him from revealing what he knew.

Landon breathed in slow and easy as the private jet approached an airstrip no larger than a Band-Aid wedged into the only piece of relatively level terrain at the base of a ring of mountains. When they touched down, he let out his breath. No, it wasn't the swift but efficient landing that troubled him.

It was his doubts. The aliens seemed to be warning him away. Then there was Summer's relationship to them. The aliens were the reason why she'd ended up in Patagonia Prison. Maybe it hadn't been so wise to come here.

It was too late to go back. Now he had H.F.'s mission, to find the aliens' outpost.

"What are we going to find here, Molly?" Landon asked his daughter, thinking aloud, when they came to a stop and he opened the shield enclosing her safety pod. He wished he knew what H.F. had known. "Here, at the literal end of the Earth?"

"Prrrii," Molly said, trying out sounds that sprayed his face with droplets of her saliva. Then she giggled.

Greer pushed past Landon and took over with the unbuckling. "She can't talk yet. She's only two."

"We heard her last night."

"That wasn't her."

"Who was it, then?"

"Shhhh. We're not supposed to talk about it, remember? We'll discuss it later."

Landon admitted he didn't know much about children, but he thought two years was old enough to be speaking more than Greer seemed to expect of Molly. He wondered if her speech delay had anything to do with her alien resident. "I want her to be tested again," he said. "See if we can get some answers."

"Of course, Landie. Once we're back in civilization. Give me a break, will you?"

"Meanwhile..." He had an idea. "They must have a medical facility here. They would need doctors for the inmates. After all, they're not going to ship them out for medical treatment whenever a problem arises. They must have plenty of issues here."

"You want her to see a prison doctor? She's not sick."

"She seems feverish." His heart skipped a beat as his mind worked out a plan. "I think she may be coming down with something. Look how flushed her face is."

"She's been playing. Running around. Give her a chance to catch her breath, if there's any to catch in a place like this."

He gathered up their belongings and followed Greer and Molly out into the thin air, leaking sunlight. Light-headed, he glanced up at the mid-morning sun, reassuring himself that Sol was still there. He was already missing their good old sun, and he hadn't even left Earth yet. A blast of wind caught him, and he swayed on his feet, staggering down the ramp that extended to the tarmac.

At the end of the ramp stood a short, squat man, reminding him of a bulldog gone soft. He dressed in casual khakis and a loose, cotton shirt, its tails flapping over his potbelly. Two uniformed guards carrying what looked like outdated rifles flanked him on either side. The man in the center with no visible weapon pulled his hands out of trouser pockets and stepped forward in greeting.

"Welcome," he said in a mildly accented English. "Doctor

Walker, I presume? I am Raimundo Manrique, Director General of Patagonia Prison." He didn't bother to introduce his escorts.

Landon brushed past Greer to shake the director general's hand. It felt soft and flabby in Landon's firm grip. "I appreciate the opportunity to come here, especially given the circumstances and how quickly you allowed us to make this visit."

Manrique shrugged. "It was my friend Samuel who cut through the red tape to arrange your visit with us."

"Samuel?" Greer said, shifting Molly from one hip to the other. She glanced up at Landon with a puzzled frown on her face.

"Sam," Landon said with a grunt of surprise. "You mean Sam Talcott?" He wondered what, precisely, were Sam's connections to this ultimate prison.

Manrique led them to a waiting van, the old-fashioned standard kind with thick tractor treads instead of maglev supports. Its dirty-white metal frame displayed enough dents and chipped paint to suggest the van had remained in service far too long. The prison, Landon decided, received the castoffs of the world in more ways than one.

"Samuel and I," Manrique said as they settled into their seats and the van rolled away, "became great friends during his training sessions here."

"Sam Talcott trained *here*?" Landon said.

"Why not here? There are some who say our mountains are out of this world." Manrique tipped his head to one side and chuckled, apparently amused by his attempt at a joke.

The van's motion gave him a shifting, jouncing, up and down vista of snowy mountain peaks, sharply pointed. "When will I get to see Summer?"

Manrique shrugged. "I regret that your wife is out...on exercise duty at the moment. We could not adjust her schedule on such short notice."

"*Ex*-wife," Landon said. "What sort of duty?"

"We send teams of our prisoners out to build and repair roads. We have a fragile infrastructure as it is, and with our weather, roads here are in constant need of repair. Hillsides slide away, taking chunks of roads with them. Bridges wash out. That sort of thing."

"Sounds like it'd be easier to convert to maglev transportation," Landon said. They should join the twenty-first century like the rest of the world.

Manrique smiled a knowing smile, opened his mouth as if to respond, and then shut his lips tightly together, sealing his words and thoughts to himself.

Landon guessed there were other obstacles to updating the prison, and he wasn't aware of them. Maybe the constant wind battered them too much. Or maybe it was just a question of finding some activity for the prisoners, rather than letting them rot in their cells.

"When will she be back so I can see her?" Landon said. "Or should I go out to the field where she's working?" He didn't have a lot of spare time to hang around waiting for her. He wanted to get this over with.

"No, no, that will not be necessary." Manrique's voice carried a hint of anxiety. "She will return soon. In the meanwhile, we shall take you around and provide for your comfort. Is there anything in particular you would like to see?"

"Yes, actually," Landon said. "Your medical facility. I think my daughter may be coming down with some sort of bug."

Manrique's gaze snapped onto the child. Molly stared back, babbled and burped. Manrique flinched and twisted around in his seat to speak in a low voice to the driver. Landon wondered if Molly's saliva had touched the director general. Was that how the alien who used Molly reached out to control its surroundings?

Manrique turned back. "We will go there first, before settling you into your guest quarters."

* * * * *

Landon thought Doctor Chan was ill suited for her job as prison doctor, not because of her gender, since he personally knew of more women in positions of power than men, but rather on account of the blade runners she wore in place of legs. She was another example of how outdated this place was, since modern prosthetics were getting so good as to be virtually indistinguishable from the real thing. No one needed to wear metal stilts anymore, yet she had chosen runner-blade attachments. For a brief moment, he wondered why.

Then he returned to the matter at hand. His daughter. More specifically, the alien *using* his daughter.

The blades didn't seem to get in the doctor's way as she glided around the cramped but tidy examining room, navigating through her various instruments that she needed to read the chip embedded in the back of Molly's head. "Pretty necklace," Chan said, lifting a ribbon of Molly's hair from her neck and exposing the tiny golden *figa,* a fist-shaped charm the size of a baby's fingernail.

"It's a good luck charm," Greer said, perched on the end

of the examining table where she rubbed Molly's back. "Her daddy gave it to her. Isn't she a lucky girl?"

Chan smiled, looking up at Landon. "Indeed." She turned back to Molly. "You have lots of friends? Maybe one in particular that you like to play with?"

"She can't talk yet," Landon said from his hard vinyl seat tucked into one corner of the room. "According to my sister."

"We don't know that, Landie," Greer said, then smiled. "Oops."

Chan swiveled around, bringing her face a couple inches away from Molly's, peering into her eyes, still hazel. "Nothing of importance to say yet?"

"Ti-ti-ti-ti," Molly said. Then she tipped her head back, and her entire plump body bounced with the exclamation of another sound. "Nya!"

Chan reared back and fumbled her scope. The pen-shaped instrument clattered onto her datapad.

"That means 'no'," Landon said. "She doesn't have any playmates."

"Because there are no other children in the ISA compound in Goiás," Greer said. "I think it's time to move her back to my place in the Holland Annex. At least we have schools there."

That wouldn't happen, not if Landon got his way about including Molly and Greer on the mission.

Chan seemed oblivious to Landon's quibbles with Greer. The doctor retrieved her scope and touched it to the back of Molly's neck. "Titinha? Is that the name of your friend?"

"Ti-ti-ti-ti," Molly said and then finished with a burst of slobber and giggles. "Tri!"

Landon felt a cold, hard weight grip his lungs. "Nya" meant

no, he was certain, but put the rest of it together, and Molly had said "Tititri."

Just like her mother.

During Summer's trial, while her mind disintegrated, Summer had also exclaimed that word. It was the name of the aliens.

Chan frowned at her datapad. Finally, she pulled the scope away from Molly's head. Her fingers shook as she smoothed the golden strand of hair back into place. "Well," she said, clearing her throat, "Molly's stats are all normal. I can't find any microbes invading her system that shouldn't be there. In other words, she's fine. Healthy. No bugs." With her pen-scope in one hand, she rose and turned off her pad. The interview was over.

Landon expected nothing less. The alien would reveal itself through Molly only when the alien was good and ready. He hadn't expected the doctor to find it, whatever trail of evidence might lodge there, inside the child. He had another purpose for seeing Chan, and Greer, the legal guardian of his daughter, wouldn't like it.

"Doctor," he said, rising from his corner, "may I have a word with you?"

Greer slid off the end of the table and turned to stare at him, her face expectant.

"In private?" he added.

"Certainly, Doctor Walker," said Chan. "Ms. Cameron, would you mind taking Molly out into the hall for a few moments?"

"Sure, but Land —"

"Please, Greer. It's important. We'll talk later."

"You better talk, Buster, and not do your usual thing, instead. You never tell me anything. I never know what's going on." She scooped up Molly from the table and flounced out the door, slamming it behind her.

Landon wasn't trying to keep anything from Greer. It was Molly — more precisely the alien who spoke through Molly. If it was still with her, then he couldn't afford to allow it to overhear what he wanted Chan to do. As it was, he wondered if it was possible to keep the Tititri from knowing anything. No doubt, the aliens were already several steps ahead of Landon.

If only he knew their plans. If only he knew how to stop them. *Without* Summer's help.

CHAPTER SIX

GREER WALKER CAMERON PERCHED on a hard, cold bench of stone in the drafty entrance hall of the prison's medical facility. Gusts of wind rattled the double glass doors opposite her and shrieked inside through cracks.

Just the way she felt.

And where was everyone? There wasn't even a bot for a receptionist. Through the glass doors — she supposed they weren't really glass, just like all the rest of the fakeness surrounding this little mountain display of (Power? Control?) — she could see the gravel area of the inner courtyard where the van had let them out. Now, the van was nowhere in sight. The director general — Raimundo Manrique, of all the silly names — had disappeared, probably anxious to return to some cozy cubby where the wind didn't pummel him. All she could see out there instead was chipped cement walls, topped with rolls of glistening razor wire.

Talk about power!

The outer gate they had driven through was now sealed shut. Opposite that was another gate, also sealed shut. It must be an inner gate leading deeper into the prison. Towers at each corner of the courtyard were riddled with slits for watching each gate, with weapons drawn. But they were watching her. She knew it. She could almost feel the guards' eyes upon her, and their vibes sent goosebumps tickling her spine.

How would she ever walk out of here without being shot?

The door moaned as wind peppered it with a spray of grit. The cold seeped in, and she shivered, wishing she'd brought along extra sweaters in her bag. Molly didn't seem to notice the cold. Her two-year-old niece explored the tiled floor with fat little fingers awkwardly chasing down pieces of lint that skipped along like tumbleweeds in the drafty, whistling wind. She danced and twirled across the reception area until something caught her attention out there in the inner courtyard.

"Brrrr!" she squealed, pointing at the not-glass doors.

"Yes, honey, there's a bird out there. It's called a seagull. It's a long way from the sea, but then again, maybe not so far anymore, now with the oceans rising."

Molly toddled closer to the door, inspecting her friend who stared back at her. Wind ruffled its feathers and whistled inside. Molly's lips moved, trying out sputtering baby sounds.

She was so cute! So normal! So nothing at all like what that crazy woman reporter tried to make Greer believe the night before. She'd almost gotten Greer killed, rescuing Molly from those jungle women and their shaman.

The reporter claimed the baby wasn't human, just because she'd seen the DNA report.

Well, Greer had seen the report too, and she hadn't seen any such conclusion. No, it was all lies. Molly looked human enough.

Why had the reporter lied?

Why was everyone treating Greer this way?

Oh hell, she was a wreck after last night. On the one hand, Greer had saved the day, the day before, risking everything and ending up with baby Molly safe and sound. On the other hand, no one seemed to appreciate her role in the matter. And to top it off, she'd missed out on her beauty treatments because of all that excitement. Bags had tugged at her eyes all through the morning like giant weights. There was only so much that cosmetics could do.

But the real kicker was the way her brother thought he could order her around like that. *Wait in the hall.* She mimicked the words, lip-syncing and bouncing her head. Well, technically, it had been the doctor's request. But that was another thing. Her brother, the ultimate control freak, had insisted they come here, when clearly, there was nothing wrong with Molly.

Nothing wrong with her DNA report, either.

Greer's frazzle smoothed out as she watched Molly jabber at the seagull. It flew away, and then her niece held out her arms to either side and flapped them while toddling a few steps away from the door. She was imitating the bird! What a smart girl.

Greer sniffed and dabbed at the moisture forming in one corner of her eye. Damn wind was going to ruin her make-up.

"Where are you going, honey?" Greer said. If only Greer's pals back home from her body sculpt club could see her now. Who would've ever thought a year ago that Greer, of all people, would end up caretaker to her brother's baby?

Landon. Who did he think he was? Another Sam Talcott?

Screw this. Why in hell had he dragged her here to this wind tunnel in the first place?

It was all because of that top secret mission Landon was involved in. *That* didn't add up, either.

At least she knew now that her first suspicion was correct: it was all about aliens. A shiver rippled down her spine as she watched Molly pause and peer down a hallway leading off this reception area without a receptionist. "Come back here."

Molly turned to look at Greer. She seemed all right, at least at the moment. Her face was a baby's face, with plump cheeks and disproportionately baby-like features.

No more green eyes, thank god. That woman's face — the woman with emerald green eyes — sometimes shone through, surfacing from inside Molly's face as if she were a mysterious eight ball.

The aliens did that. Greer didn't know how. Maybe the green-eyed woman *was* the alien. Although, her image that floated around, just under Molly's baby skin, certainly looked human enough. If it was an alien face, it had porcelain-doll features that Greer would die for.

No one asked her, but she suspected it was because the aliens were trying to reach out to them. Trying to talk to humans. Too bad they'd chosen baby Molly as their medium. She hoped that was just a mistake on their part, and not because Molly was special. Being Summer's daughter, who knew what the baby could be? And Landie's, too.

Landon, she meant.

Greer sighed. They were supposed to find out here in Patagonia, weren't they? If Summer had anything to do with why the aliens wanted baby Molly. *Had* wanted, she should say. It was over now. After last night. It was, wasn't it? She shivered again. Sweat chilled on her skin.

She couldn't help but wonder... What *really* didn't make sense to her... If that mission to Proxima Centauri was all about aliens, then how had they managed to keep it all so hush-hush? Why was that reporter last night the only one who'd found out about it? She imagined news like that would go viral. It would be impossible to contain.

And another thing... Why would the mission go *away* and leave Earth *unprotected*, for god's sake, wide open for the aliens to come and take over? She'd seen enough movies. That's what aliens did, wasn't it? Why wouldn't Earth create a master plan, instead, to unite everyone to stand up and fight off the invading aliens?

Why didn't they put someone in charge who knew what he was doing? Not Sam Talcott. He couldn't be trusted.

Although surely, he must have some sort of plan. No one was telling Greer, that's all.

An image of tall, suave, slightly graying Sam danced enticingly through her memories.

God, that body! And to think, he almost... They almost...

She pushed the lust from her mind and sprang from the bench, hurrying down the hall after Molly. "Honey, wait for me!"

Greer didn't trust that man. He lied. The day before yesterday, he'd led her on, making her think he actually *wanted* her. The truth was that he'd conspired with that jungle woman, Ziza, to kidnap Molly, and all the while he was distracting Greer with empty promises.

Greer caught Molly's hand and squeezed her closer. But Molly resisted, squirming with a sudden yank of her hand and slipping out of Greer's grip. Her niece darted away with a giggle, and Greer gave chase. This game was better than sitting idle in the middle of a wind tunnel. The chase broke down into baby steps, allowing Molly to gain distance.

Given the amount of closed doors and signs with weird symbols, Greer wondered if they were supposed to be here. Well, too bad. No receptionist had stopped them.

One door stood open, and Molly darted inside. Greer followed, stepping into a pocket of cold air. Shivering, she noticed the rows of drawers lining one wall, similar to the cryo-ward back in the Holland Annex where she'd enrolled in beauty treatments a time or two. Or three.

But this place was different. It wasn't all body drawers. The opposite wall contained built-in electronics, humming and blinking colored lights, and studded with buttons and knobs and levers and several flashing screens. She didn't think they were supposed to be here, whatever this place was.

"C'mon, Honey, let's go back. They'll be looking for us any minute." She picked up the child and turned to go.

The door to the hallway swung shut with a click of its latch.

CHAPTER SEVEN

MINUTES TICKED BY IN SILENCE AS Landon stared at the closed door of the examining room, wondering how secure it was. The back of his neck tickled as he felt Doctor Chan's attention on him, waiting, probing his mind.

Finally, she broke the silence. "Did you want me to change the dressing on that wound of yours?" She nodded at the bulge on his shoulder, pressing against his dress shirt.

"It's fine," he said with a grunt. "Just a nick."

"Molly isn't the real reason you wanted to see me, is it?"

"She's a good reason, don't you think? We can't have her sick at a time like this."

"But she isn't sick," Chan said, folding her arms across her white, formless lab coat. "Tell me what is so special about this time that you can't have her sick right now. Is it about your mission?"

That got his attention, and his chin jerked around to meet her gaze. "You know about that?"

"Of course I know. This may be the bottom of the Earth, but we don't live in a vacuum down here. We get Worlds News, like everyone else."

"Ah. Then, you saw their report about the Centauri mission?"

She nodded and grinned. "You bet. The first ever manned mission to another solar system. That's pretty exciting stuff. It should finally launch soon, shouldn't it? Once everyone finally assembles on the Orbiting Launch Platform? You don't want Molly to miss all the excitement, is that it?"

"That's part of it. Mainly, though, I want you to remove her tracking chip."

Chan narrowed her eyes to black slits. "You have permission for that?"

"Not in my hand, but it's on the way, I have been assured." Landon felt heat rise up his neck from his lie, and he swiped his hand across his buzz cut. Chan assumed he was Molly's legal guardian, just because he was the father. Let her think that.

"Those chips are standard equipment in children under the age of twelve," Chan said.

"I know. But trust me, this is a special case."

"Some of us in the medical community fought long and hard for those children's chips. Not only do they locate the children, should they become lost for whatever reason, but also they monitor their changing health requirements. Sometimes exemptions are allowed, but really, in my opinion, those chips should stay intact even longer, perhaps through young adulthood, until the brain is more fully developed. You will have to wait for your authorization before I can consider your request."

"I can't wait. This is too important." He couldn't tell Chan his suspicions about the aliens, that they were accessing his daughter through her chip. Aliens were a far larger matter than the question of sidestepping the law.

Chan shifted, bouncing atop her blades, and regarded him

with a frown. "Why here? Why now? Why not wait until you get the permission in hand? You can have it done back in Goiás."

He shrugged. "I like to be as efficient as possible, doctor. When we return there, we will be occupied with final preparations for launch. We are here now, in a holding pattern, waiting idle for the return of your prisoner, my ex-wife. You could do the procedure while we wait. Why not get it over and done with?" His gut burned with the acid of his thickening lie. The truth was, he didn't want to see what else the aliens could do, besides deactivate a steward bot.

"I wonder," Chan said, tapping her index finger against the thin, unamused line of her lips, "if this unorthodox request of yours has anything to do with my interviews with your ex-wife."

"You're seeing Summer professionally? Then, you do psychiatry as well?"

"No," Chan said. "Why I see her is public record. I can tell you that much. Her speech disorder is not classified. Summer Jeunne-Walker hasn't spoken one coherent word since she entered this facility."

"That's not true," Landon said. "She spoke to me over a call I placed here, only last week." His blood chilled at the memory of her words:

It's started, she'd said. *We tried to warn you, but you wouldn't listen.*

No, there was nothing wrong with Summer's voice. Chan couldn't convince him otherwise.

Prepare... Summer went on to say. *Don't let them take her. Teee-teee-treee... We are Tititri... Don't let them take Molilia.*

He hadn't understood Summer's warning, not then, not until Ziza — the Amazonian woman who'd infiltrated ISA

— kidnapped Molly two days ago and took her to that cult of Mundomba women. He still didn't understand how Summer had connected herself to the Tititri in the first place, and then had also gotten Molly mixed up in whatever scheme they were concocting. How had she done that from the confines of her prison here in Patagonia? Nor did he understand how the Mundomba figured into all this business about aliens. He didn't understand what it was that had "started," nor what anyone had to prepare for.

Only two things were clear to him: some conspiracy of crazies were after Molly, and Summer was playing all of them for the fool. He would demand answers once he saw her, and then he and Molly and Greer would get the heck out of here.

"Trust me," Landon told Chan, "Summer can talk."

Chan tipped her head sideways, rippling her hair like a black curtain. Doubt shone clearly from the frown lining her face. "I am testing her for any possible medical cause to her speech disorder."

Landon snorted. "Her problems are all mental. Look, there must be a recording of my conversation with her."

"Yes, I've listened to it," Chan said, lowering her voice to a whisper and blinking furiously.

"Then you heard her speak."

"It wasn't speech that we could recognize. She uttered nothing but nonsense syllables." Chan stared at him, defying him to contradict her.

He opened his mouth to protest — he'd heard her *words* — and then clamped his jaw shut. If nonsense was what the recording revealed, then it was only his word against...solid evidence. Contrived, obviously, but solid all the same. If he protested too loudly, they would consider him as unreliable a source as Summer. But he'd heard her. He'd heard the warning. He didn't understand it, but he'd heard the words. If Summer's actual words hadn't been captured on the recording, or if her words had been garbled somehow, then something mechanical had clearly malfunctioned. As the steward bot had failed within range of Molly.

Chan continued to evaluate him thoughtfully. "You interpreted meaning from her nonsense syllables." It was a statement, not a question.

He turned away from her penetrating gaze and studied the array of bins that held various instruments. Was it possible that instead of hearing Summer speak to him, it had been the *alien* speaking through Summer? The same way one of the aliens had spoken through Molly? Was it possible that only the intended receiver could interpret the sounds? One of ISA's linguists had tried to explain it last night in the jungle when the alien spoke through Molly. The linguist believed that the alien's communication came through in whatever language the receiver understood.

Only one week ago, Landon wouldn't have accepted any of this. But now he couldn't deny what he'd seen. What he'd heard.

"What did Summer say to you?" Chan said.

"You're right," he said. "It didn't make sense." He didn't know yet if he could trust Chan enough to tell her his theory. But what he said was true. The words hadn't made sense, although he'd heard the words spoken clearly enough. Definitely not nonsense syllables. If Chan hadn't understood the words, then Chan wasn't the intended receiver.

Chan sighed. "All right. *I'll* tell you what she said: 'Tititri'. The rest, we could not decipher. I was hoping you might've understood the rest of it." Chan paused, giving Landon an opportunity to explain. He didn't, and she went on. "Some of our, um, research indicates that 'Tititri' is a sort of code. It seems to be used among our prisoners."

"Research?" Landon asked, lifting an eyebrow. Chan was clearly dancing around some information she did not wish to share.

"Does that surprise you? That we conduct research in a facility such as this?" She folded her arms across her chest, body language that dared him to question her.

"Not really. Depends on the research." He swept one arm around him, encompassing the bleak, mountainous setting for a maximum-security prison. "Your research probably probes the minds of your inmates under these conditions, I'm guessing."

"Partially. Communication is your field, correct?"

He shrugged. "Not on a micro level, such as you're referring to."

"I'm not talking about that. I'm talking about 'Tititri'. Why did Molly say it, too, just now?"

"If you're asking me, I don't have an answer for you." He wasn't going to tell her about the aliens. That was still classified information.

"I wonder," she said with a skeptical tone of voice that suggested she thought Landon was the one who suffered mental problems. "I have to tell you, it was a bit of a shock, hearing *that* word come from your daughter's innocent lips."

"What's your theory? What do you think the code means?"

"Death."

Landon's lungs clenched. "Death?" He managed to spit out his question.

She nodded. "All on account of your Centauri mission. You go, and we die. Like —"

"Like what?" Like the deaths that had already surrounded preparations for the mission, so far? Collateral damage, they'd told him back in Goiás. But now he wondered what it all meant. Icy waves of dread crashed through him. The Tititri aliens meant death.

"Like a signal," she said. "Your mission is a signal that will generate massive uprisings. And death."

H.F. had thought the signal meant imminent death, too. But Chan was guessing. She didn't know about the aliens. "What makes you call it 'my' mission?" No one was supposed to know about Sam Talcott's offer, but everyone seemed to know. Landon hadn't even responded to the offer with his counter-offer.

Chan narrowed her eyes at him. "You're going on the mission too, are you not?"

He coughed to cover up his irritation that speculation seemed to decide for him, before he'd had a chance to negotiate his terms. He changed the subject again. "Hopefully, Summer will tell us what she knows, and that will clear up all of this business about Tititri."

"Good luck, getting her to talk to you."

"She'll talk. She has to."

Chan assessed him with a skeptical twist of her lips. Then she turned away from him, as if deciding against saying whatever else was on her mind. She gathered up her tools and dropped them one by one into their storage bins. Her voice mumbled as she worked. "Maybe I made a mistake."

More likely, he thought, someone had leaked classified ISA information to her. "How well did you know Sam Talcott when he was here, training, or whatever he was doing?"

She ducked her chin, but not quick enough. Landon saw the flush ruddy her cheeks.

"Ah..." he said. "Pretty well, eh?"

She spun on her blades and rose to face him, defiant. "I don't know that what I do in my personal time is any of your business, Doctor Walker."

"It isn't. Sorry. But help me out here, please. Certain details of that mission are classified information. We suspect there have been some leaks, and we need to know how that's happening."

"Is that why they sent you here?"

"No."

"Well, you're wrong about Sam, if you suspect him of being your informant. But yes, he did call to tell Director General Manrique and me that you are to be a last-minute replacement on the mission. That is why he urged us to allow your visit on such short notice. That is all."

"I don't think that's all. If you've heard mention of Tititri *and* you know about the mission, then you must help me." His heart thudded, and he lurched on his feet. "Please, doctor. Remove the chip from Molly. Set her free from all this Tititri business. That chip is what's causing it."

She chewed her lower lip, then shook her head. "I cannot. Not without the proper orders."

Landon let out a loud sigh of frustration. "How could I possibly leave for twenty-four years without ensuring my daughter is free from danger? Surely, you can understand that."

Her chestnut brown eyes softened. "Yes. I *do* understand." She sighed and finally continued. "There is someone else who may be able to help you. Someone who is not bound to the Worlds Court. He is known around here as El Pastor. That's not his real name, of course, but it is true that he has a way with primitive medicine, using local roots and leaves and whatnot. He tends goats and lives in a hut high in the mountains not too far from here. Unconventional, I know, but he has some healing powers we can't deny, just because we don't understand them. We haven't analyzed the chemical components of his poultices and teas, but his process is more than that. There's an element of...oh, call it his 'bedside manner.' Over the last several months, I persuaded Director General Manrique to allow him to visit some of our prisoners, so that I could begin that analysis and study his procedure. He succeeded with most of our patients, except for the one I was most interested in, Summer Jeunne-Walker. Even though he could not restore her speech, his success rate with the others was impressive."

Chan was suggesting he allow some medicine-man goatherder to take a *scalpel* to Molly's chip.

His horror must've drained the color from his face, because Chan laughed and said, "Don't worry. If anyone can interfere with Molly's chip, it will be El Pastor and his poultices. I'll give you the name of one of our guards who will guide you to him." She pulled a pad from her pocket and shook it, but it was already awake, flashing a message at her.

She frowned as her eyes tracked the message.

"Something wrong?" Landon asked.

She looked up, erasing the frown with a smile. "No. Nothing at all."

65

CHAPTER EIGHT

WITH HER HANDS FINALLY UNCUFFED, Summer swung the pick, lifting it above her head and landing it with a thunk into the boulder-ridden ground. The roadbed they were constructing dropped down from the mountain pass and crept closer to the glacier.

By now, the cold had numbed her fingers, wrapped around the handle, and frozen her joints in brittle lock-place. Her shoulders burned from the rhythmic motion. She was a living and breathing model of fire and ice. If anyone could call this living. Or rather, she was scarcely living.

She was biding her time, powerless in this place, waiting for the Earth wars to begin, when the Tititri would take control. And then what? It would mean the end of human existence. For her, the sweet release from the hellhole her life had become.

But Diamond had said they each had a job to do, as if he had access to some special information. He'd hinted *she* was someone special, but he was wrong. Within Patagonia Prison, the information flow was sketchy at best. She was no one. No one to the Savers. He, on the other hand, was a renowned assassin, far higher up in the Savers' network.

Her body followed orders, feeling as buried and frozen inside prison routine as whatever lay buried beneath those tin tree trunks poking out of the glacier a hundred meters or so away. That's where the road that they were building seemed to lead. To the glacier.

Pebbles splintered loose from the ground and sprayed the air as she worked, side by side with Amazon, Diamond, and the couple dozen others along the line of shackled prisoners. Not all of them had been given picks to work with, only random selections that included her, despite the injuries from her fall. What did the guards care? They had been torturing her with their whips and chains ever since she arrived in this place, a timeless length of never-ending time ago. Those inmates without picks scooped away chunks of loosened rock and dirt, shoveling them to the side and pounding the new roadbed flat. Pieces of the rocky mountainside escaped their piles, rolling and tumbling down the slope into the valley far below. Even up here, high above timberline, Summer could hear the murmur of the river down there, swollen from eroding glacier.

"*Sque-e-e-e-e!*" cried a bird from somewhere overhead.

Guards snapped their whips at the prisoners' heels and aimed rifles at their backs as they worked, a reminder not to even think of turning their tools into weapons. Even if anyone tried, the shackles that bound their ankles wouldn't let them flee very fast. Even if any prisoners managed to escape, they had nowhere to go. They could not survive in this inhospitable land of desolation.

Summer swung again and again, her motions controlled by the rhythm of dull, thudding sounds, whacking away, little by little, at the frozen ground. *Thump whump thwack.* A sense of timelessness descended over Summer, and she became an automaton, wound up to go on aching and thumping forever.

Chink!

The echoing ring of metal on rock inserted into the battering sounds, breaking the rhythm of thuds. One boulder the size of her dead baby's bed wouldn't be dug out. Up and down the line of prisoners, swinging arms fell still.

Larger boulders and drop-offs wouldn't allow their road to go any other way. The guards motioned the prisoners away with their whips and rifles, pushing them closer to the glacier. Some of the guards stayed behind to set dynamite charges in the troublesome area of rock.

Diamond, beside her, uttered an oath and rolled his shoulders, shrugging them around the steel cord of his neck.

Tickles skittered along Summer's spine as the guards herded them towards the glacier. When they'd moved far enough away from the blast area, the whip snapped. They dropped their picks and shovels and sank wearily to the ground. The guard with the whip and another guard with a rifle positioned themselves on either side of the circle of inmates. The rest of the guards remained behind at the rock area, setting charges, where most everyone's attention riveted.

Not Summer's. She studied the three tin tree trunks. They were neither large enough for a skyscraper building nor extensive enough to form part of a buried city, as she'd originally thought. Maybe it was a house, instead. Except...

Up close, she could see that the exposed tips were rounded pieces of dull gray metal, not a golden halo at all. The metal didn't glint and shimmer in the sunlight, not even as the glacier did. She supposed the buried thing wasn't a house, either. A metal house? Metal told her it was a machine. Whatever, it was some sort of metal contraption, which meant it was artificially produced. It was man-made.

Even her frozen mind recognized that something man-made couldn't have found its way *under* a glacier. These glaciers had been here for hundreds of thousands of years, long before humans could've forged anything from metal. She didn't think humans had even been around that long.

But someone had put it here, on the side of the mountain, to be buried under layer upon layer of snow, each layer freezing over eons of time.

We did, said someone.

Summer glanced over at Diamond. "You did what?"

"Nothing yet," he said with a grunt. "My target ain't here yet."

"You keep blabbing about the Savers," said Amazon, "and your target will never show up."

Summer glanced above Diamond's head, at the sky, where a bird flew past the visible wedge of moon that floated over the mountains. That's where the voice had come from. This time, and all the times before.

Diamond and Amazon were wrong. It wasn't the Savers who spoke to her anymore, not after they'd urged her to do the things she'd done that had landed her in Patagonia Prison. At first, she'd thought it was the Savers, but after thinking about it over time — for, what else could she do in confinement but think? — she realized that it couldn't possibly be the Savers. Her voice spoke to her when the moon was out. How could the Savers speak to her from the moon, when space travel was one of their causes they fought against? No, it couldn't be the Savers who spoke to her from the moon.

Someone...some*thing* that lived up there on the moon had

buried its metal machine down here, under the glacier eons ago.

Ice gripped Summer's lungs. Trembles rippled along her spine.

Some*thing* alien had invaded her head, speaking to her from the moon.

CHAPTER NINE

THE SLICK, METAL DOORKNOB slipped uselessly in Greer's free hand. It wouldn't open. "Hello?" she called, pounding on the door, clutching Molly to her hip with her other hand. "Is anyone out there?"

No one responded. She couldn't even hear the soft whir of the door's inner machine, operating things behind the scenes. Of course, as outdated as this place appeared to be — and why would it be anything but outdated in a place like this? Did prisoners really need the latest, the bestest of the best? — they probably didn't even *have* electronics inside doors or behind the walls. After all, there were plenty of computers and who knew what type of machines already exposed in plain view in this room. And besides, there'd been no reception bot.

If there had, she and Molly wouldn't be here, locked inside this creepy room, would they? A bot would've stopped them from wandering away from the bench where they were clearly supposed to wait. They wouldn't have gotten accidentally locked inside some machine room, with a solid wall full of what looked like body drawers.

So cold in here.

It wasn't Greer's fault for wandering away, chasing Molly down the hall that led to this room. No, it was the bot's fault that it hadn't been there in the first place to keep this accident from happening.

It was the absent bot's fault that the door had somehow locked or otherwise jammed shut. And now she and Molly were trapped.

Greer cast a glance behind her at the wall of drawers as she leaned hard against the metal door that would spring them back into the hall. Holding Molly in her arms gave her added weight, but still, the door wouldn't budge. She felt panic rising from the pit of her stomach up her throat.

She wondered who, or what, lay inside those drawers. Each drawer was square with a single, centered handle of cold steel, and the dimensions looked just large enough to hold a human body. It looked like one of the walls of the anti-aging treatment center back in the Holland Annex. Did they do something similar here? Were there bodies inside these drawers? Were they preserved in cryo-storage, or...

Was this place a *morgue*?

Goosebumps crept up and down the back of her neck at the thought of being locked inside a room with a couple dozen dead people.

Why not? This was a prison, so she supposed the bodies were not here for beauty treatments. Why would they preserve the *dead* bodies of murderers? Why not just toss them over the side of the mountain, into the chasm far below? Let them wash out to sea? Who would want to reclaim the bodies of murderers, after all? Who would mourn them?

Why didn't someone open the damned door for her and let her out of this chamber of horrors?

She didn't want to convey to Molly her mounting alarm, and

so she put on a happy face. She felt her smile stretch her face, especially around her ears, reminding her that she sometimes missed spots there when she applied her daily anti-aging ointment.

She looked back at the wall of drawers. It was only one wall. Weird machines filled the rest of the room. Humming and swooshing and burping, some of them were built into wall sockets, while others sat on counters and portable carts. They weren't like any electronics she'd ever seen before, not that she was an expert like her brother. These machines were probably some sort of modified computers. There were gray metal boxes that sprouted spinning bobbles and quivering poles and whatnots in addition to wires and monitor screens. Instead of displaying dull squiggly lines the way most monitors did that Greer had seen, these showed interesting kaleidoscopic patterns. Shapes shifted, looking like little starburst splotches of red and blue that stained across the screen.

These machines must be used for some sort of experiments. Chan's experiments, she would bet on it.

Wait a minute. Experiments meant that some tech person would eventually come back to check on things, right? All she and Molly had to do was wait.

A wave of relief swept over her, knowing they would eventually be discovered before dying of hunger or thirst. She only hoped he or she would find them before grumpy, grouchy Landon came looking for them.

And what a story she would have, telling him about this room.

Feeling emboldened, she marched over to the wall of drawers. It was important to convey to Molly her sense of entitlement. No fear. They belonged here. More than that, their presence claimed this space as theirs. If they owned this space, then they needed to know just what the hell was going on here.

She wanted to see for herself that they were bodies. Or not. She really hoped not.

Molly kicked against her thighs, indicating she wanted down. Greer wrapped her arms even tighter around the child. "Not now, Honey. There's a lot in here that you mustn't touch."

But Molly squirmed harder. And when Greer reached for the nearest drawer, Molly slid from her loosened grip and dropped to the stone floor with a thunk. She toddled away, heading towards the thrumming machines.

"Wait, Honey." In mid-reach for the drawer, Greer turned quickly to recapture Molly. The sudden switch made her lose her balance, and Greer stumbled while Molly sped away.

"Priiii," Molly said, glancing over her shoulder.

Her eyes... Oh no. Her eyes glowed emerald green. The way they'd done the night before. When that alien woman's face shone from inside Molly's face and spoke through Molly's lips. But Greer thought that was over. It couldn't be happening again.

Molly had hazel eyes, and hazel eyes changed color, depending on the lighting. That had to be what Molly's eyes were doing now. The colorful lights of the machines must be affecting her eye color. It wasn't the alien. It wasn't. Not again, *please*. Not now. Not here.

"Honey, this isn't a game."

Molly raced on, toward the machines, which suddenly clicked and fell silent. The blinking lights, the colorful patterns all disappeared, all at once. The bobbles stopped spinning, the whatnots stopped quivering, and the gray metal boxes looked dead.

Greer leapt after Molly, before the child could touch anything. She hadn't touched anything yet. She hadn't. The machines had just stopped working all by themselves. They were probably programmed ahead of time to turn off at this precise moment. Or maybe they were deactivated remotely. She didn't know. But she *did* know that Molly hadn't done anything.

Another click sounded behind Greer, just as she caught up to Molly. She picked up the child — the green eyes were gone, faded back to hazel, thank god — and turned around. The locked door to the hall had opened, and a man stood there in the open doorway. A hunk of a man.

"What's going on in here?" he said, one hand holding what looked like a gun, aimed in her direction.

CHAPTER TEN

"I'M SORRY THAT I HAVE TO leave you now," Doctor Chan said, but Landon thought she didn't sound sorry at all. "A robot guide will take you to your quarters, will that be satisfactory?"

Landon nodded glumly, following her through the door of her examining room. His footsteps echoed down a sterile hall, and her blades swished as she led him into the reception area. It was empty. "Where are my sister and daughter? Why didn't they wait for me?"

Chan shrugged. "Sometimes children can't wait. Don't worry. Your driver must've taken them to their quarters."

He wasn't worried.

He didn't like to beg. He'd begged with Chan back in her examining room just now, and it left the taste of humility stuck in his throat like a sour belch.

But he wasn't worried.

Chan activated a spider bot, which crept out of its wall crevice, snapped into a track in the wall, and whirred away, around a corner to another hall. Landon thanked Chan and set off, following the bot to a stairwell. It led down into damp tunnels beneath the medical facility.

This bot was one of the older guide models, headlighting the concrete arches before him as he made his way along passages from the medical wing to what he hoped would be the residential sector for prison personnel. At least this equipment was not as old as the van that had brought them here from the airstrip. Most important, the bot still functioned, guiding him eventually to a lift at the far end of the tunnel.

Even more distasteful than the memory of his begging Chan was her refusal of his request. He wasn't surprised, but he'd had to try. What he hadn't expected was her counteroffer to let some local goatherder do the job for her with his medicine man potions.

Rubbish.

He left the spider bot behind in the tunnel as he stepped onto the lift. Linked to the bot's program, the lift carried him up, and when the doors whispered open, he stepped out into blinding sunlight. The sudden flash from dark to light made him stumble, which sent new flares of pain to his shoulder wound. He blinked furiously to allow his vision to settle.

He stood on an enclosed bridge connecting two corner towers. A bubble of fortified transparency covered this uppermost level and creaked under the strain of the wind. The birdseye view of the prison layout below showed him how the stone block of the prison, embedded within double walls, jutted out from the side of a mountain. Peaks soared above his head, and at the very top, patches of snow reflected searing light. Canyons dropped below his sight, leaving him dizzy from a wave of vertigo.

"Ah, there you are," said a man's slightly accented voice from behind him.

Landon turned to see Director General Manrique slouching in a doorway that led into the interior of one tower. His personal guards were gone, but given the network of doors clustering around the lift, Landon suspected the guards weren't far away.

"Chan said you were on your way." Manrique motioned for Landon to follow him.

Landon hesitated only a moment and then stepped briskly after the director general. Evidently something had come up to delay his rest in his quarters. He suspected it had something to do with that message Chan had received after turning down his request to remove Molly's tracking chip. The message had clearly disturbed her.

He followed Manrique through a series of anterooms, each one staffed by a scowling employee and outmoded tabletop electronics. Above each door glowed the pinprick of a camera eye. Through the open doorways Landon glimpsed their apparent destination, a much larger and more plushly outfitted office.

It was a corner office, with windows overlooking the world outside the prison. Landon glimpsed a single road far below, winding up the narrow canyon from the airstrip to the outer gate of the prison.

Inside, Manrique closed the door to his office, clicked its lock, and pressed his palm against a metal plate in the wall. A line of bubble lights flashed from red to yellow to green, spreading like a wave of green security across the panel. Manrique tapped a sequence into a keypad, and the green lights blinked off.

"Now we can talk freely," he said with a sigh. He waved Landon into an armchair and added, "I trust everything is all right with your daughter?"

"Under control at the moment." He didn't feel as confident as the tone of his own voice implied.

Manrique nodded. "If your daughter is under the weather, Doctor Chan will find out why. She finished her training in the Holland Annex before coming to us, so you know she's one of the best in her field. She knows what she's doing."

Landon shifted, crinkling the vinyl cushions of his chair. "I hope you're right."

"Don't let those blades fool you," Manrique said. "She wears them like a badge of honor, in memory of her parents who died saving her in the crash of their personal cart. They saved her life, but they couldn't save her legs."

"Why would she want to be reminded constantly of a tragedy like that? Can't she put it behind her? Doesn't that get in the way of her operations?"

Manrique shrugged. "I can understand your concern, given your wife's residence here with us."

"*Ex*-wife. Summer's a prisoner, not a resident, and what does that have to do with Chan's choice to wear blades instead of modern prosthetics?"

"An unfortunate comparison, perhaps." Manrique waved circles in the air, as if smoothing out Landon's unsettled thoughts. Then he lowered his voice, even though the blank lights by the door indicated that he'd turned off any surveillance equipment. "We don't always understand the choices others make. You must wonder why your ex-wife chose to give up her freedom."

"The only choice she made was to join that terrorist organization. The Savers." Or possibly the aliens, as H.F. suggested. Either way, she'd been brainwashed. He was positive. "She broke the law, and now she's paying the consequences. The law sent her here."

"Do you not wonder sometimes," Manrique said softly, as if probing Landon's mind, "why she made the choice in the first place, her choice to break the law, as you phrase it? She would've known the consequences."

Landon frowned. He'd known her well enough to feel certain there had been no free choice. She had been forced. Something had happened during his absence, on his voyage to Titan. If he hadn't have gone there, maybe none of this would've happened.

There it was. His guilt. Greer was right. They'd come all the way down here to Patagonia for him to assuage his guilt. Because he couldn't leave on a twenty-four year mission without first cleansing himself of his guilt. But he didn't know how to accomplish that, short of breaking Summer out of prison.

He didn't want to face his shortcomings, so he changed the subject. "I need to place a call to Goiás, to ISA headquarters. Do you have a secure link I can use?"

"The only one I know for sure is secure," Manrique said, "is right here in my office. I will set up the link for you in a minute, but first we must talk about the real reason you are here."

The back of Landon's neck crawled. Either Manrique knew about H.F.'s holo message or Chan had told him something. He tried to keep his voice even. "Simply, I'm here to visit Summer."

Manrique waved his words aside. "We know that is not the real reason. We have called you down here because we need ISA's help."

Landon stiffened. He had made the initial request to come here. No one else had made the decision for him. His mind spun, trying to reconstruct his conversation with Sam, when he'd put in the request.

"In fact," Manrique went on, "no one can help us better

than the space agency. Not when it comes to aliens, don't you agree?"

"Aliens?" Landon sputtered. But then, he shouldn't have expected news about aliens to remain quiet. Word had leaked out.

"You see," Manrique said, "we believe that aliens have not only visited Earth. They have arrived. Perhaps they live among us. It is critical that we understand their intentions. You, as ISA's representative, will know how to proceed. You must help us."

CHAPTER ELEVEN

ZIZA FONSECA NO LONGER felt her feet, caked within blocks of mud and woven with bits of dried palm fronds. She could not find a patch of her flesh the size of a fingernail that did not contain a bite mark. Bumps and mounds of swelling from her bites distorted her body, changing its surface into a washboard. The itching nearly drove her crazy, but she had stopped scratching hours ago when the parasite within her told her to stop peeling away her flesh.

She'd stopped batting away the armies of gnats and bees and beetles that buzzed her face and now stuck out her tongue to catch them. She'd seen Mãe eat all kinds of bugs during lean times of hunger. The bugs did not stop Ziza's hunger pangs, and sometimes they stung the back of her mouth, but at least they would keep her from dying straightaway.

Whoever, whatever tracked her through the jungle should have killed her by now. It could've overtaken her, but hadn't. It toyed with her. Perhaps it was only a curious tribesman, wanting to know what she was up to. She wished she knew herself. She did not know where her feet carried her.

Or maybe it was one of Mãe's women, looking out for Ziza, who'd spent too many years away from the jungle, in the re-education camps down south. The doctors there had tried their best to sponge Ziza's jungle upbringing out of her and turn her into a citified woman. Maybe it was one of their people who followed her now, feeling guilty for having left Ziza helpless upon her return to the jungle. It was a meager attempt at compensation for having used Ziza and tossed her away like a fish's skeleton.

Ziza did not know the way. She did not know where she headed. The mud blocks of her feet seemed to know the way, and she just went along for the ride. She had never been in this part of the jungle before. She did not recognize the flow of the river she followed. She had not passed another soul along the river from whom she could ask advice and directions. Although, she did not know what she would've asked had she found anyone to ask.

She should have killed the little girl. It would have been the easier way. She did not understand why the boss of her boss had wanted the child returned unharmed to Mãe's people. She could still do it. If she found it. It was here, somewhere. She would find it. Killing it would release her from the mud blocks of her feet.

CHAPTER TWELVE

"OH!" SAID GREER, STARTLED more by the hunkishness of the man rather than the gun he aimed at her. She squeezed Molly tighter in her arms. "It's about time someone came to let us out."

The hunk leaned against the door into the hall, and it snicked shut behind him.

Her heartbeat did a little dance. "You can put that thing down," she said, twirling her index finger at the gun. This time Molly clung to her like a baby monkey. With her movement, the gun lifted a titch higher rather than lower, much to her annoyance. "We're not inmates, you see. We're guests."

"I know who you are," he said in a low, throaty voice, on the verge of a growl. His focus flicked from Greer's eyes to Molly's face and finally to Greer's boobs. Meanwhile, his broad, muscled shoulders held the weapon steady throughout his eye tango. Not even a quiver showed. "What are you doing here?"

"We got lost." She nodded at the wall of body drawers. "What is this place, anyway?"

"It's not on the tour." Finally, he lowered the weapon. "What did you touch, to make the monitors turn off like that?"

"Nothing, I swear." Neither had Molly. "Stuff just went off, all by itself. There must be a remote control center somewhere, right?" Why was she explaining this to *him*? Obviously, he knew. He was just harassing her.

He evaluated her curves with the iciest blue eyes she'd ever seen. They glittered like blue diamonds against an olive complexion, which didn't go together, in her opinion. She cocked her head sideways, contemplating his mystery.

"Who did you say you were, again?" she asked with a flirty lilt to her voice. Mysteries always attracted her. And attractions always reminded her how long it had been since... God, she was so horny.

"I didn't."

Oh damn. That approach wasn't going to work with him. "Well, I just thought... Since you said you know who *we* are... We should know who *you* are." Her gaze dropped to his lowered weapon, and her attraction instantly evaporated. "Jesus Christ, did you really mean to *shoot* us?"

"I do what I have to do. And so should you. You can't go wandering into areas that are off limits. There are simply too many dangers in a place like this."

"Such as what? What dangers? What *is* this place?"

"Classified."

"Then, why was the door open, inviting us in?"

"I do not know." He moved swiftly across the room toward the dead machines and punched a sequence of buttons. Nothing happened. His frown deepened.

Molly stiffened and jerked hard against Greer's body as she twisted around, following his movements.

He jabbed at more buttons and turned some knobs, but the gray screens remained stubbornly gray. The power buttons kept sleeping. He cursed under his breath.

"What's wrong?" Greer asked, shifting her grip on the child to clutch her tighter.

He kept scowling at the machines, rather than looking up at her. "What did you do?"

"Nothing. I already told you. But I was about to do plenty if no one came to let us out. Tell me, why did that door close all by itself and lock us in here?"

He ignored her and lifted his left wrist to his mouth. Eyeing her, he spoke softly into his wrist com, summoning someone, a tech she supposed, to come and check out things in m-oh-thirteen, whatever the hell that meant.

It meant that she would have to find another way to remind him of her presence, to make him listen to her and maybe even answer her questions. She bet she'd get his attention if she checked out whatever was hiding behind those body drawers. While he was otherwise occupied, she marched over to the wall of drawers and reached for a handle.

"Hey!" He shouted at her and leapt across the room faster than she could move. He grabbed her by her reaching arm and twisted until she cried out. "Don't touch that."

"Why not? Is it going to bite me?"

"It might. Besides, it's none of your business. You want to get a permanent passport into this place?"

"Are you threatening me?"

Before he could respond — not that she thought he would — a voice crackled out of his wrist. It sounded like meaningless gibberish to Greer, but it must've conveyed some sort of coded meaning to the hunk, as he stiffened, listening.

Then his gaze lowered onto Greer, and the hard line of his jaw softened. As he contemplated her, the ice in his eyes thawed to pale puddles. He seemed to have run out of retorts. A thrill coursed through her, dancing on the edge of forbidden fire. And she'd won.

"They're waiting for you at dinner," he said.

"Dinner? At this hour? Don't you mean lunch? And what about my room? What about —"

"Come along. I'll escort you. You don't want to be late for dinner."

"Well, I guess I am a little hungry, now that you mention it. And I'm sure Molly is, too. But we're supposed to wait for Lan — I mean, my brother."

"I'm afraid he's been called away."

"Away?"

"Yes. Rather suddenly."

"Oh. Summer must be back, then?"

"I wouldn't know about that. Come along, if you please. This way."

What an odd man. First he locked her in here, ready to shoot her in an instant, and now he was kicking her out. And what about her guest room? Couldn't she at least freshen up a bit before dinner? She must look like something the cat dragged in.

CHAPTER THIRTEEN

LANDON'S PULSE POUNDED AT Manrique's plea for help. The director general fell silent, but the weight of his words left the air in his office heavy, suffocating, and hot. Landon felt oxygen-deprived. The stiff vinyl of his armchair crackled as he pushed himself to his feet. He towered above Manrique's bald spot shining with beads of sweat.

"What makes you think aliens are here on Earth?" Landon said, frowning. He'd had a similar conversation with H.F. only a few weeks ago, another of the life-long arguments they'd carried out. He'd thought it a game, humoring the old man and his pet theory. He should've known better. H.F. had been right. Again.

"On account of the artifact we found," Manrique said. "The locals knew it was here all along. Then Doctor Chan started working with some of the indigenous folk a couple years ago in her clinic, building up trust between them. Eventually they revealed the artifact's presence to her, although they didn't know what it was. They considered it a sacred spot of their ancestors."

Landon paced to the window. He wished he could crack it open and get some air to clear his head, but there was no handle, and the window sealed him in. He felt lost. Helpless.

He couldn't help anyone else if he didn't know how to fight aliens. "You've seen it?"

"Yes. It is true."

"You think it's alien. Why? What kind of artifact is it?" *An outpost*, H.F. had said in his holo message.

"We believe it's a spaceship that crashed."

Landon grunted and scanned the mountainous landscape outside the window. Somewhere out there, according to H.F., aliens lay dormant.

The Tititri won't stop until they've taken all of Earth, he'd said.

They were dormantly *dead* in the crash of their spaceship. That had surely stopped them.

But the Tititri were neither dead nor dormant. Landon had heard one of them speak through his daughter. He turned away from the window, waiting for Manrique to go on. When he didn't, Landon prompted him. "A spaceship? Why do you believe that? Have you examined it?"

"Not personally, no." Manrique pulled a handkerchief from his pocket and dabbed it to his brow. "Doctor Chan and her team are working on finding a way to access it."

"How did she conclude what it is, then? Are you sure it isn't a piece of our own equipment? Something left over from one of the early space programs? Maybe a downed spy satellite?"

Manrique smiled and refolded his handkerchief. "Buried under a glacier?"

Landon felt a weight press on him. His knees weakened, and he grasped the slick windowsill for added support. *The Tititri have been here longer than any of us ever suspected...* That's what H.F. had said in his holo message. Surely he hadn't meant *that* long.

Landon shook his head, not understanding. Maybe he and Manrique were talking about different aliens. After all, the wreckage of a spaceship could not possibly serve as an alien outpost. The ship would be dead. Like the aliens who'd piloted it. "Let me get this straight. Your artifact, a crashed spaceship you think, has apparently been here a very long time, perhaps pre-dating the rise of humans. Why is that a threat to us *now*? Why are you concerned about alien intentions? Didn't your aliens die a long time ago? And how do you expect ISA to intervene?"

Manrique held up one hand and patted the air, steamy from Landon's confusion. "I know, I know. I will do my best to answer all of your questions. Bear with me, please. Soon after the discovery, I reported it to my boss from the Association of Worlds. Let their agents, the Executors, deal with it, that's what I thought. Maybe the artifact was booby-trapped. There had to be a reason why the locals hadn't interfered with it. You see? The Executors responded by bringing in a team to investigate."

"Then, why do you need ISA's help?"

"Because the Executors aren't talking to us. And Doctor Chan is convinced that the artifact holds some sort of power over the indigenous people she works with."

Landon snorted. "Whatever it is, alien or not, it's not magic."

"Of course not. Although, as someone famously pointed out long ago, that which we don't understand can sometimes appear as magic. When the Executors completed their investigation, they told us what they believed, that it had indeed come from a crash, but not from a spaceship. It's a leftover from war days, maybe a missile. A missile would've penetrated the ice, burying itself deep."

"But you don't believe them. Why not?"

"Because of what happened after the Executors left."

"They left?"

Manrique nodded. "They designated the site classified, and then they went away."

"They closed the case on it?"

"Exactly."

"They didn't leave someone behind to secure the site?"

Manrique shrugged. "They brought in a new warden for us. But before he arrived, Doctor Chan reported that the spaceship — or missile — while it may have crashed, is not entirely broken. There are some sort of machines aboard, and she detected a power surge from them."

Landon sucked in his breath. "When was that?"

Manrique stroked his chin and gazed at the ceiling. "Let me see. Last winter. Around the end of July or early August?"

When the signal came through. When Landon collected the emission on SpaceHab. When the science station at Valles Marineris blew up. When the image of the sphinx came through. When Van Pelt hanged himself and left his note of a single word: Tititri.

The signal was meant to arrive when the time was right to awaken the Tititri from their dormancy and begin their invasion. That's what H.F. had said. Had the old man been right again?

"Did the Executors or Chan find any...uh, alien remains?"

Manrique shook his head. "Nothing. Or at least, the Executors are not saying. They reported to our board about the mechanical equipment, and after bringing in more people to study it, they declared it nonfunctional, not a threat."

"But you and Chan disagree."

Manrique shrugged. "Something caused that power surge. Are the shipboard machines trying to contact their home world? It's imperative that we know their intentions."

"Shouldn't you contact the Executors again? Let them handle it?"

"Yes, of course, in due time. But first, I would like some answers. The Executors made it clear that they are not in the business of giving answers. I think they are not in the business of alien matters, either, not as the International Space Agency must be. So, I called my old friend Samuel, and he promised he would send someone. You."

Landon swiped one hand across his buzz cut. Sam hadn't sent him. Sam knew he was already planning to come here. As had H.F., as if the two of them had conspired together. "I'll see what we can do. What about that link you promised to set up for me?"

* * * * *

Some moments later, Landon sat alone inside Manrique's office and faced the wallscreen. This office wasn't cutting edge enough to include a holo pit. The director general had set up the link to Goiás and then left, giving him privacy. The bubbles on the deactivated control panel by the door remained colorless as he closed the door behind him. No one in an ante office out there was monitoring him.

Landon wondered how secure the prison's system could

be against aliens. He watched the wallscreen, which showed Sam Talcott, the acting interim director of the International Space Agency. A large bear-shaped man, he was little more than a washed-up astronaut, trying to take over H.F.'s role, but with none of H.F.'s panache. He paced and fumed within the windowless confines of H.F.'s office. Sam had taken it over as his own, prickling Landon with annoyance.

"You didn't tell me that you've been here before. That you and Manrique are old buddies." And maybe Chan.

"You didn't ask," said Sam from the other end of the link. "Have you thought anymore about what we discussed last night?"

That's all Landon had done. He wanted to go on the mission, but he didn't see how it was possible. "You are already fully informed of the situation down here, then? You know all about Manrique's claim? About the artifact."

Sam sputtered and pushed his thick fingers through the waves of his salt and pepper hair. "Not entirely. That's why you're there, to fill me in."

"I'm here on personal time," Landon said, frowning. "But Manrique seems to think *you* sent me. And H.F. left me a pre-recorded message about my coming here. He knew all about it, too. Why am I the last to know? What's going on?"

Sam stopped pacing long enough to scrutinize the camera, as if he could peer through its lens and into Landon's head. "Message? Where is it? That's ISA property, and you need to turn it over."

"You'll get it. When I return." Landon leaned back in his chair, imitating a relaxed pose to cover up the tension he felt. The data stick was still in his travel bag, unless Manrique's guards had already searched his gear and removed it.

"Tomorrow. We need you back here tomorrow." Sam resumed pacing.

"That may not be possible. I haven't seen Summer yet. She's out on some sort of exercise duty. I have to wait for her return."

"How much longer?"

"They won't say."

"You don't have that long," Sam said. "We've got a schedule to meet. I need your commitment now. And I need you back here tomorrow. Otherwise, I'll have to find someone else to fill your seat on the Centauri mission."

Sam didn't have any other candidates to replace Landon, and he knew it. Landon had built the tachyonic equipment. No one else knew it as well as he did. Sure, he'd trained the crew to use it for basic communication purposes, but no one, not even Landon's closest associate in his lab up on SpaceHab, could make the necessary adaptations this mission would require. He was supposed to track the aliens who'd sent the emission.

"I may need more than a day," Landon said. "ISA is required to give me personal time for extended time served on a mission. It's in the contract. H.F. put it there in the fine print." Sam was so new that he probably hadn't read it yet.

Sam sighed. "Anything else you require, doctor?"

Landon felt his mouth twitch into a brief smile. Sam's desperation was enough to give a cautious man like himself some leverage for negotiations. "I'll let you know."

The wallscreen fell heavy with stillness. Sam's face flushed and his brow creased. Blackness clouded his eyes. His lips moved silently as if he were doing some mental calculations.

The timing of the schedule, no doubt.

Sam finally spoke. "If you're worried about your kid on account of Ziza and her jungle tribe, you can forget it. They won't try anything again. And even if they do try, they won't be able to get inside the compound. They can't get past our security."

"Not like she did before?"

"That was different. She was one of our employees then. Look, don't worry. Your kid is gonna be safe here in Goiás. Safe from Ziza."

"Maybe so." *If* Molly stayed behind on Earth without him, but that wasn't going to happen.

"You can't waste anymore time," Sam said. "Leave the kid down there with Greer. They can stay behind and wait for Summer. Wasn't that the whole point of your little trip to Patagonia? To reunite the kid with her mother?"

Landon swore under his breath.

"Look," Sam said, "we need you back here. The commander is getting anxious. She's ready to rock and roll. We need you on that last spaceplane up to the launch platform."

"I haven't given you my answer yet if I'm even going."

Sam muttered through his teeth. "Don't crap out on me now. You're going on the mission, we all know that. Just say yes, and cut the crap."

"I still have a couple of other things I need to do first. A couple of things I need to figure out."

"Such as?"

"Let's start with H.F. He knew about the artifact, didn't he?"

"It's a long story, and you don't have enough time to hear

it. What else?"

Landon startled with surprise by Sam's refusal to answer. Maybe the link wasn't as secure as Manrique thought it was. He remembered how H.F. had always spoken in code, fearful of hackers listening in. "I'm working on it." If Sam wasn't going to be forthright with him, then Landon could be equally evasive.

Sam snorted. "You'd better work fast. You've got until tomorrow. Is that clear? I want you and my equipment back here first thing tomorrow."

Landon bristled. First of all, the shearjet wasn't Sam's personal property but ISA's, built with H.F.'s funding. Secondly, Landon didn't feel any allegiance toward Sam. Let Sam fire him. Maybe that would be for the best. Landon's primary obligation was to Molly, after all.

Even so, he wanted to find a way to do both, to protect Molly *and* go on the mission. He hated to have to choose. "We'll talk again tomorrow."

But he couldn't promise that it would be in person.

CHAPTER FOURTEEN

THE AIR SURROUNDING SUMMER exploded with a boom, pounding her eardrums and rattling her teeth. The ground shook beneath her, and a cloud billowed up, peppering blasted bits of rock into the air. Coughing, she choked on the dusty taste of pulverized granite and covered her ears with the palms of her hands. The circle of prisoners huddling with her, halfway between the blast area and the glacier, gasped and muttered oaths. Even the two guards with them coughed and wiped their eyes.

Summer felt herself shaking long after the sounds rumbled away and pebbles rained back to the earth in a fine mist of sand. Either the ground continued to shake or she did. Then a new sound, like the crack of a whip, split the air. She looked up from the shield of her arms, but the guard with the whip had not flinched, not even a muscle. The air cracked again, a sizzling pop of static electricity, and the ground vibrated.

"Shit," Amazon said, staring in the direction of the glacier.

Summer followed his gaze. The glacier roared as a chunk of ice split away from the main flow and crumbled into hundreds of pieces, spilling down into the canyon far below.

"This is it," Diamond said. "Now's the time."

Hurry!

The wind howled around them, carrying shrill cries on the currents. It was a woman crying. Not Summer. Shivers rippled through her, like a cancer eating away at her soul. She felt one with the wind woman's pain. She felt her loss. She *was* her loss. She felt her hopelessness aching through her, cell by cell. Aches for the life that had never existed. The promised life that nevermore would be.

Nothing but death surrounded her. She didn't know why she persisted, but persist she must. The future depended on her. On *her* alone. She was the special one. Even Diamond knew it.

What did the future matter? Without the hope she could offer? They were lost. She was lost in the vast, wasteland of time. She was as lost as her baby and husband were lost to her. Had they ever existed?

It was time. Past time. Time to seek the new home. A backwater place where they would be safe from the invaders.

Safe. Almost there.

Muffled grunts rippled through the prisoners beside Summer. "What is it?" someone said.

Questioning voices murmured through the chain of others and awoke Summer from whatever trance had snared her. She startled as someone shoved her aside, lunging for her pick, where she had dropped it beside her feet.

"Gimme that," Amazon said.

A guard cried out, and a whip snapped against their heels, entangling the threesome. Amazon snarled, throwing his giant shape into the swing of her pick, breaking Diamond's shackles with a clanging snap and a crunch.

Echoing sounds answered from the glacier. Metal creaked,

ripping apart. Guards shouted.

Summer's mind spun, following the rapid-fire sequence, leaving her dizzy. The whip sliced her ankles with fire. Amazon whirled around, hurled the pick into the air, in the general direction of the guard at the other end of the whip. A thunk sounded at the same time as the guard cried out and fell backwards, the metal blade of the pick lodged in his chest.

Then Diamond grabbed Summer, lifting her off the ground. She felt herself being tossed around, shifting in Diamond's grip, bouncing against his back as he ran with her, slung across his shoulders. Upside down, she watched the group of prisoners recede behind her. The air exploded in *rat-tat-tat* gunfire, and she watched Amazon fall, a felled giant.

Amazon, shot! *No!*

She pounded against Diamond's back, but he did not slow. Rifle shots zinged past their heads as he zigzagged onward, gaining distance. A bird flew alongside them, soaring through the air.

The prisoners and the guard with the rifle disappeared from view as darkness enfolded her in a tomb of cold air. Diamond bounced to a stop and huffed, taking several deep breaths. He shifted her again, swinging her from his back and twirling her around into the cradle of his arms. The smooth wall of ice that sheltered them brushed against her clawing hands, its touch searing her like fire. Her face spun around, aiming into the raw wound of the glacier. It was a cave of ice, an opening left behind by the chunk that had split off moments ago. Thin sunlight filtered through the wall of ice, breaking down into a gloomy illumination of a dark wall at the end of the rift. There was no escape. But then, she had known that.

Diamond kicked one booted foot against the wall. The dangling ends of his broken shackles landed with a clanging thud. "They said it'd be here."

This wall was the buried base of the three tin tree trunks, she realized. She faced the metal contraption that the voice from the moon had buried here, under the glacier.

Come.

The bird chittered. Shouting voices and thudding footsteps grew louder behind them while a layer of metal peeled away from the wall before them and curled up above their heads. A hole, or perhaps a door, opened into the darkness. A puff of warm air spurted into her face through the hole in the side of the machine. It smelled like...a cross between...some chemical... bug spray? And something organic, like decay laced with a sweet, cinnamon edge.

"Can you see anything?" she asked Diamond. "I can't see inside."

"It's dark as tar," he said with a grunt. His arms shifted around her again as he tipped her head towards the hole. Arms and hands scrabbled to shift their grip along her body, bruising her flesh as he rammed her into the dark interior, into the warm, putridly chemical air that filled her lungs. One last shove, and the world rocked around her with a deafening roar. Its thunder vibrated through the dark, shaking the air enfolding her. She slid down... Down...

CHAPTER FIFTEEN

THIS WAS MORE LIKE IT, GREER thought. A small sigh of delight slipped through her lips as she sank into the plush cushions of her chair at their table set for six in the staff dining room on the uppermost floor of one of the towers. The other tables weren't laid out as finely as this one, with linens and china and best of all, crystal wineglasses. In fact, none of the dozen or so other tables were occupied at all.

All this, just for lunch!

The heads of department lived in luxury, treated like royals, if they lived like this, but she guessed they needed some sort of benefits to attract them here to the end of the earth. The scenery was gorgeous, too, starting off with the blue-eyed hunk who'd pulled his gun on her. He sat opposite her now, keeping his attention focused on her, as if she'd completely swept him off his guard. She didn't mind that eye candy. Behind his broad shoulders, a wall of windows framed the storybook scenery of soaring mountain peaks and sheer cliffs, dropping off into the chasm of a gorge so far below that it appeared bottomless.

Behind her, the door out to the hall slapped open. She twisted around in her seat at the familiar click-clack sound of Landon's footsteps. He strode quickly into the dining room, leaving Director General Manrique behind in the dust of her brother's impatience. "Here you are," he said, on the warpath to her side. "At last." Her brother was always in too big of a rush. He would end up with a coronary one day if he didn't slow down.

"Where on earth were *you*? This guy said you'd been called away." She nodded at her nameless bodyguard, whose blue gaze iced over, inspecting Landon.

"I am afraid the fault is mine," Manrique said, catching up, a little winded. He pulled out his chair at one end of the table, next to Doctor Chan, who was talking in a low voice to one of the servers. "I took him away from you for a little consultation."

"Consultation?"

"Never mind, Greer," Landon said with his annoying big brother tone of voice. He gave Molly a quick squeeze and sat down next to the highchair, which thankfully buffered Greer from him. "What happened to you?" he said, peering around the toddler's tray. "Why didn't you wait for me?"

"Molly decided to take a walk, and I couldn't let her wander away by herself, now could I?"

"You must never wander anywhere on these grounds without an escort," said her bodyguard with a frown. "You could find yourself in serious danger. Our guards have their orders. Shoot first, ask questions later."

"So, you're saying we were lucky *you* found us in that room instead of one of the guards?" Greer fluttered her eyelashes. "What was so important about that place, anyway? You never told me."

"Correct."

"Listen to him, Greer," big brother said.

She ignored him. "What's in those drawers? Some of your inmates?"

An uncomfortable pall of silence fell over the room as her escort, Doctor Chan, and Director General Manrique exchanged significant glances. They couldn't hide the fact that they were trying to hide something, whatever was in the drawers inside that room, Greer would bet on it. They'd probably been doing unspeakable experiments on inmates, experiments that had gone horribly wrong. That was surely why they didn't want anyone to know. She made another mental note and turned to her brother.

"Landon, you're a machine guy. I'll bet you'd like to see that weird equipment, except it probably wouldn't look so weird to you. You'd understand why it's all so hush-hush."

"Not now," he said, his voice harsh.

"I am afraid it is no secret," Doctor Chan said with her smug smile. "We merely keep specimens in there, for our research. We conduct research in that wing, and with some of the chemicals we store, it's not safe for anyone other than lab personnel."

Specimens, right. Greer bit her lip to keep her thoughts bottled up inside, thanks to Landon's scowl. Human-sized specimens, that's what she bet they were. And what about the burping machines that looked like giant kaleidoscopes?

"The door should not have been open," Doctor Chan continued, "and I apologize on behalf of my staff that it was. I shall find the reason for that infraction, you may count on it. I shall get to the bottom of this."

"I would be very interested in learning more about your research," Landon said.

Manrique gestured sweepingly at the window. He lifted his voice to a high-pitched level of cheer and changed the subject a little too obviously, in case there was any doubt, which there wasn't, that they were trying, but failing, to hide something. "Work is good for our prisoners. Especially hard labor out of doors. Isn't that so, Doctor Chan?"

A seagull swooped across the view out there, and Molly squealed, pointing at the window. "Birrrr!"

The doctor laughed at the interruption. "Quite right, Raimundo. Studies have found a direct correlation between physical labor and morale."

Landon perked up, asking about those studies, but while they techno-babbled, Greer pieced together the other snippet of information she'd garnered. That woman doctor had called the director general by his first name: Raimundo. They must be an item. Greer mentally filed away the interesting piece of information. You never knew when you might have to draw from that store of information that always went over Landon's head.

Her bodyguard drew her out of her mental note taking and leaned close to the table. He stretched his arm across its width — no gun, anymore, at least not visible — and spoke to Greer, almost in a conspiratorial whisper. She thrilled to be included in anyone's conspiracy. "Are you part of the crew on the spaceship to that other star?" he said in his low, throaty voice.

"Me?" A single laugh erupted from her, making the others pause their conversation long enough to glance at her. "Do I look like an astronaut?" What made him think *that*? She shook her head.

The others resumed their intellectual discussion, and her escort went on. "But your brother is going, yes?" His gaze was intense, the way it bored into her against the background chatter.

"Oh, no, of course not," she said, sucking in her breath, caught up under the spell of his attention. She couldn't help herself, even though this man had been prepared to shoot her only a short while ago. Male admiration always made her glow. "My brother is just part of the team up in Goiás, who have to direct things from Earth. He has a daughter to think of, y'know. He can't leave her."

He tipped his head sideways. "Do they really expect to find a habitable world, as the news reports suggest?"

"How on earth would I know?"

He leaned back in his chair, withdrawing his hand from the starched white linen of the tablecloth. "You're here, are you not? Surely, you are skilled with special knowledge. Why else would you come along on a trip like this, from the top of the world down here to the bottom of the world?"

His sudden switch in interest from Landon to her made her tingle all over, starting from the tips of her toenails. Yes, she felt special, and skilled. Definitely. She warmed to the new topic. "Because of *her*." She smiled at baby Molly strapped upright in the highchair between Greer and Landon. "He won't let this little girl out of his sight, not after what happened last night."

"Ah." Her admirer smiled with secret understanding, as if he'd been there. But of course he hadn't. "And what happened last night?"

"I'm not supposed to talk about it," she said, feeling a thrill ripple through her. He was literally pumping her for information! Information she couldn't explain, even if she was allowed to talk about the aliens. "See here, are you implying something else? You think I know more than what I know?"

He shrugged. "I imply nothing. Children are no concern of

mine. I am much more interested in you. You appear far too young to be saddled with the care of a child."

Greer wanted to bristle. His denial of implying anything actually implied an attitude that demeaned children in general and Molly in particular. He was wrong. Absolutely, one hundred percent wrong. But he thought she looked young? That trumped everything else, and she babbled on, a geyser of information. "Landon says the reason why we've come here is more than just about seeing Summer."

"Oh?"

Well, well. Mr. Ego didn't believe her. That was clear enough in the tone of his voice, the skeptical rise in pitch. He didn't think she was smart enough to have any information worth knowing, did he? She would have to prove him wrong, without getting herself in trouble by giving away what she knew about the aliens. Not that she knew anything. "He thinks there's something here. I heard him tell the baby so."

She glanced at Molly, who moved her lips and stared at the window, as entranced as if she watched a movie. "Talking to your friend again?"

"Birrrr!"

Greer laughed and dug through her bag for the tin of biscuits she usually carried for food emergencies. She offered one to Molly and then looked up at the nameless man, but he had turned his back to her. He faced the mountain scenery and whispered into his wrist device. Even so, she overheard a few swear words and noticed the tightening of the muscles across his back.

"Something wrong?" she said.

"Nothing." His chest rippled as he turned back around and

tapped his wrist. "You were saying what it is that you expect to find here?"

"Not me. Him." She glanced over at Landon, who was deep in conversation with the woman doctor. When she turned back to her own admirer, she noticed that he was watching Molly — not Greer — with as much fascination shining from his rugged face as the look Molly gave to the swooping, soaring antics of her seagull. So. Not interested in children, was he?

Greer clicked her tongue and said *ahem*, trying to recapture his attention. "My brother won't tell me what he thinks, of course, but I can guess. It's something linked to the...to Molly." To the alien, she'd almost blurted out. "Whatever it is, it drew her to that room where you found us."

That got him. He lifted one eyebrow. His gaze darted to Molly and then back to Greer. "I am afraid you are wrong. You must get that room out of your head. There is nothing of importance there."

Nothing but aliens, she thought, biting her tongue. *Shit!* That's why Molly was drawn there. *Aliens!* Not dead bodies of inmates, not human-sized specimens, but alien bodies. That's what was in there. And this guy *knew*. That's why he wanted her out of that morgue and machine room.

Okay. Breathe, Greer.

She took a deep breath, forced back the retort that wanted to bubble forth, and said instead, in as mockingly pleasant a voice as she could muster, "Tell me, what is your official capacity here? What do you do, here at the prison?"

Besides monitor aliens.

"Nothing with babies, I can assure you." He snapped his fingers at one of the circulating servers who carried two wine bottles and gestured at Greer's empty glass.

Well, that was a conversation killer, Greer thought as she studied the vintage and chose white. She noticed that the irritating man who avoided answering her questions covered his own glass with his palm, as did Landon. But she expected that of her brother. She hadn't seen him take a sip of the bubbly since... Goodness, was it at his wedding? Back when Summer still seemed relatively normal. Before the aliens messed her up.

"How is Summer Jeunne-Walker fitting in here?" she asked, unable to imagine. The man still hadn't identified himself, but she presumed he must have some dealings with the prisoners. If he was at this elaborate luncheon, then he must have some position of importance. She couldn't imagine her sister-in-law in a place like this.

"This is not summer camp here, Miss Walker. As I said, there is a lot of nothing here. Nothing of interest to be found. Now, back to your brother's mission —"

"Cameron," Greer said with a sniff of satisfaction. The irritating man didn't know everything, did he? "My last name is Cameron."

"Yes. Okay. Miss Cameron —"

"But you can call me Greer. And you are...?"

His frown softened, not quite to a smile, maybe closer to a sly grin. "Do they really think they will gather any data that is worth the danger they will surely encounter on such a mission?"

"Oh, I get it," she said. "Will you show me yours if I show you mine?"

He frowned again, this time looking puzzled instead of angry. Maybe he didn't understand. She would have to spell it out to him. "Look, I'm not going to say another word until you tell me what's so important about your specimens."

He continued giving her a puzzled frown as the techno-babble between Landon and Doctor Chan ended. Or at least, Greer hoped, their conversation paused long enough for the servers to begin their service. Director General Manrique raised his glass of wine.

"To our guests," he said. "Welcome to Patagonia. May you stay on this side of the bars." He chuckled and took a sip of his red wine.

Greer's skin crawled at the thought of being on the other side of the bars in a place like this, perched on a ledge overlooking a drop into a bottomless chasm, surrounded by fields of ice. There was nothing here, as her escort had so emphatically said. There was no escape, even if they left the bars wide open. She shuddered.

Greer noticed that Doctor Chan also sipped red wine, and for a moment felt scandalized. Well, why not? If she was head of the medical department she probably shuffled paper around rather than filling syringes. That she had seen Molly a short while ago was an exception. An excuse, maybe, to see her brother. Was that why they'd banished her and Molly from the examining room?

She glanced over at her brother, who was chatting quite smoothly with the woman with no legs. God, were they *flirting*?

Greer hoped there were no medical emergencies later in the day, after this wine-infused luncheon, but even if there were, Doctor Chan must have an underling on duty, allowing her to wine and dine with VIP guests. Thrill rippled along Greer's spine at the thought. VIP! That was her. But the irritating man across from her didn't seem to impress. He also wouldn't partake of the party. Just like fuddy duddy Landie.

Landon, she meant.

Greer turned her attention elsewhere, to their host, Director General Manrique. Raimundo. She smirked with secret knowledge.

"How many prisoners do you have here?" Greer said pointedly at Raimundo Manrique, trying not to sound like a tourist, but rather an interested party. She wanted to join the conversation, even if she risked slipping up about the aliens. Landon would kill her, if she did.

Raimundo turned to the mystery man. "Well, Warden? What are we up to now?"

The blue diamond eyes glittered and the brow scowled. "Down to, more likely. We lost one today, out on exercise duty, so that brings us down to seven hundred thirty-six."

Landon grunted. "What do you mean, you lost one?"

So. He was a warden, was he? The warden turned his icy gaze onto Landon and shrugged. "Conditions aren't shall we say, the best out there. Occasionally we lose someone. Sometimes to the cold. Sometimes to a fall."

"You mean, they escape?"

"Never. You might call it release, but there is no escape, I assure you."

Raimundo interrupted the exchange. "Allow me to introduce our warden, Brant Hermanson. He came to us three months ago from the Holland Annex. The best people always come from there."

"Oh really?" Greer said, ignoring the intended compliment. "You might've said something. After all, I *do* know more than just a few people there." She'd brushed shoulders with lots of the sciencey types, over at the facility her body sculpt club frequented.

Brant the warden, her personal bodyguard, shrugged. "Not in my circles."

She wasn't buying it. "So, answer your own question: what brought *you* down here, from the top of the world to the bottom?"

"A job. An assignment. The prisoners. Same as you."

Landon interrupted. "One of your prisoners died out there today?" He nodded at the massive glass wall, displaying mountain peaks. She wondered if the glass magnified them or if the peaks really looked that monstrously intense.

"Probably," Brant said.

"But you don't know for sure?"

"Not precisely."

"Why not?"

"There is no body."

"Your prisoner could still be alive."

Raimundo Manrique cleared his throat and waved at the mountains, in case Landon had missed noticing their towering presence. "Rugged terrain out there, plus conditions, make a rescue attempt dangerous. Very risky."

Landon ignored him and kept drilling the warden guy. "You know who it was? What are you doing to find your prisoner?"

"There is not much we can do until we learn more details, and that won't happen until the rest of the group checks back in, perhaps as soon as tomorrow morning."

"They stay out there overnight? Is that wise? In conditions like that? Don't temperatures get down around zero?"

"Are you questioning our methods, doctor?"

"Not at all. I'm asking for information."

"You won't get that from him, Landon," said Greer. "He wouldn't even tell me his name."

Blue-eyed Brant laughed. "Forgive me. Here, we do not have much occasion to practice our social skills. I'm afraid we don't have much use for good manners. We fall out of practice."

Good manners had little to do with social skills, Greer thought. Or practice. Why were the most attractive men always the ones with fewest manners? Like that Sam Talcott was. Well. She'd learned her lesson with *him*, hadn't she?

"Is it normal," Landon asked, "for your prisoners to stay out in the elements overnight when they go out on exercise duty?"

"It is not unusual." Raimundo Manrique jumped in again, since the warden wasn't succeeding in convincing Landon. "As you can see, the territory is quite extensive. For them to accomplish anything at all, sometimes they have to travel great distances."

"So they camp along the way?" Landon's face turned dark, which meant anger. Greer knew that dark look quite well. She wondered why he cared. He was done with Summer, after all. She *thought* he thought Summer got what she deserved. At least, that's what he claimed. Maybe not. Was *that* why they'd come here? Did Landon have some secret plans to spring Summer from jail?

Greer stiffened. If that happened, then Greer would lose Molly to Summer. Not legally, but still. Now that Greer'd cared for the toddler these last nine months, she couldn't imagine life without her anymore. And to think how nervous she'd been when that courier had brought her as a baby — special delivery, wink wink — to her apartment in the Annex. She'd never had any experience with babies before, and desperation charged through her. She'd *had* to accept, because how on earth did one *ever* defy an order from the Worlds Court? If you did, you'd end up in a place like this. Not Patagonia, but just as desolate, and a prison all the same. Patagonia was reserved for those who wanted to blow up Earth. She shivered. How could anyone want to destroy their own home, just for some misbegotten belief? Some stubborn principle?

She stared out the window as Landon argued with Brant about the conditions overnight. Clouds were gathering across the peaks, swallowing the sun. Gray, angry clouds. Great. She hoped the approaching storm wouldn't leave them stuck here at the end of the earth.

CHAPTER SIXTEEN

ALL THROUGHOUT THE MEAL, Landon had seen Greer's bedroom eyes bat and flutter at the warden, Brant Hermanson. His sister couldn't manage more than five minutes without her hormones driving her. He shuddered, picturing his daughter under his sister's sole influence for the next twenty-four years, without Landon around.

If Sam had his way, that's what would happen, while Landon chased alien signals across the universe.

He couldn't do it. Couldn't let his daughter grow up that way. He couldn't leave Molly and Greer behind, unsupervised. And Sam, unqualified as he might be to fill H.F.'s shoes, would never be persuaded to Landon's unorthodox terms.

He wanted to take Molly and Greer along on the mission.

But Sam would never allow it. Landon knew he wouldn't. He could tell from the tone of Sam's voice over the link. His body language, too. Landon would never be able to persuade Sam to his terms. Sam might concede and agree to add Molly, but never Greer, especially not since Sam had also come under the power of Greer's bedroom eyes. And how could Landon go with Molly and not Greer? Legally, he couldn't. Anyway, he couldn't take care of a baby, not without someone's help.

Landon was back to square one. Which meant returning

to his original, more reasonable plan to prevent the aliens from accessing Molly.

As the meal ended and the diners sat for a moment, under the quiet cloud of settling the nourishment, Manrique rose from the table and broke the air of contentment. "I suggest we all return to our posts."

Hermanson scraped his chair back and stood. Landon scrambled to his feet and intercepted him halfway to the door. "May I have a moment of your time, Warden?" Landon said.

Hermanson paused long enough to glance at the other faces studying them, and then dipped his chin in what Landon took as agreement. He marched on toward the door.

Landon caught up with him outside the room, in the hallway that bridged two towers. "You said it was a guard who gave you the information about the prisoner you lost out there today."

"Correct." Hermanson kept striding down the hall. Landon matched his stride.

"I would like to speak to that guard."

"Impossible."

"Why?"

"Quite simply, he's not here. He rotated off duty."

"Is that your usual practice?" Landon said with a frown. "Send someone out on an overnight exercise duty even though he is scheduled to rotate off duty?"

"Still seeking information?" Hermanson said with a twisted smile.

"I need to know if the prisoner who was 'lost' was her. Summer."

"You can relax. It wasn't her."

Landon didn't relax. He wondered how he could convince

the warden of his urgency without telling him about the aliens. If word about the presence of aliens leaked out to the rest of the world, there would be mass uprisings of panic, far greater in scale than the events of the night before. If H.F. was right, and Summer knew where he could find the aliens' outpost... He had to find her.

Hermanson tipped his head sideways, studying Landon. "If you'll excuse me, Doctor?" The warden turned on his heels and clicked away.

Landon caught up to him again. "One more minute, please. Manrique says you came here from the Holland Annex, but there are no prisons there. Only the headquarters of the Association of Worlds. Is that where you worked?"

Hermanson shrugged. "Everyone is a prisoner in the Annex, a prisoner to the habitat. Leave the protection of the habitat, and you die."

A bit dramatic, Landon thought, but the man had a point. "So you knew the residents there, same as you oversee the inmates here? Is that what you're trying to tell me?"

"I tell you nothing. You surmise."

"You've been here three months, which means you must've been in the Annex at the time of Van Pelt's death." Landon was certain he caught a flicker of a grimace of recognition at the mention of Van Pelt's name. "Did you know him?"

A shadow passed across Hermanson's face, as if he was doing a mental calculation, realizing his recognition of the name had been discovered, and now he couldn't deny the knowledge, the possible association, and how much could he continue to withhold information from him?

"I might have heard of the case," Hermanson said slowly.

"A researcher who took his own life?"

"Correct. Did you know him? He was a colleague of mine, and I think he may have stumbled across a significant... uh, discovery, which might help explain the motive behind his death."

"In forbidding places like the Annex, one needs no motive for death."

"Van Pelt was the sort who was always so caught up in his work that he would not notice his surrounding circumstances. I doubt he would let any depression about his surroundings take over his life and allow such depression to end it for him. Instead, I think he found out something, perhaps something he was powerless to control."

"It is unfortunate about your colleague," Hermanson said, turning away. "But I hardly see how that is pertinent to the loss of our prisoner on exercise duty. Now, if you'll excuse me."

Landon caught up to him again. "If you worked with the Executors in the Annex, then you had access to Worlds Court and their file on Summer. I want to see it." He had to know the circumstances of her being sent here, within range of the aliens' outpost.

"You *want*? That's a tall order, Doctor."

"Can we just cut the red tape? If you know for a fact that Summer is still out there with the rest of them, then you know where she is. You need to bring her back here as soon as possible."

"What's your rush? They're scheduled to return in a day or two."

"I don't have that long. I have to be back at ISA headquarters in Goiás by then. I have to see her before I head out. It's imperative. For all of us."

Hermanson paused his march along the hallway and glanced askance. One eyebrow twisted. "Surely you exaggerate."

Clearly, Hermanson didn't understand the nature of Landon's meaning about imperative. "I'm afraid not. It's a matter of grave urgency for the entire human race."

Hermanson scoffed. "All of our inmates are a danger to society, but you can rest easy. They are put away for good here. Our security system is state of the art, even if the rest of this place doesn't look it."

"If it is so state of the art, as you claim, then how is it that you manage to lose prisoners?"

Hermanson folded his arms across his chest. "A special team is assembling now to search for the missing prisoner."

"I'm going along."

"We cannot allow that."

"You cannot stop me. If you won't bring her to me, then I will have to go find her."

CHAPTER SEVENTEEN

ZIZA FONSECA RETREATED DEEP within her own body. She no longer felt the mud blocks of her feet. Nor did she feel her aching muscles or her blisters, protesting this flight by foot. She no longer felt the itch and sting of the bug bites covering her flesh. She did not even feel her flesh or the slapping swish of fronds as she plunged on through jungle.

Someone else felt all that now. Not Ziza Fonseca.

"Jun-gle?" said the other one's voice through Ziza's lips. Someone else had taken control of her body. It was not her voice, and yet, it sent vibrations through her entire being.

The voice tickled Ziza in this dark, wet place where she had retreated. She felt pleasantly buffered, gratefully at rest, as if she resided inside her own womb. Someone else's feet carried her now, gliding through wet greenness. Someone else's muscles ached and lungs inhaled thick air, dripping with the tang of herbs.

Ziza's mother used to sniff out the roots and leaves and bark that she would need for her concoctions to heal, to poison, to make fertile. Now, the other being who controlled the body once used by Ziza wished for some of that ability in this foreign place known as jun-gle.

Ziza knew what the other one wished for. She felt the last

of her consciousness absorb into the parasite, drip by drip. Up until now, the parasite had lodged within her, tingling her with its presence, driving her to make choices that she would not have made on her own. Now they'd switched places. Ziza had turned herself inside out. She had become the parasite, residing deep within her own body. Her bug-bitten exterior was the carrier controlled by the other one, no longer by her.

She was not she any longer, but they. Together, they were Ziza-Hybrid.

The Hybrid-dominant part of Ziza could use some healing power for her people. The Tititri were dying. Had died. Their world — a distant, rocky, dry world known as Ti — long dead.

Now what do we do? Ziza cried from within the Hybrid.

Ziza-Hybrid tried out her new voice, her new language, the voice she had stolen from Ziza. "We kill her. The Titinha must not be allowed to decide the fate of all our people."

The Titinha, Ziza remembered from her new nest of awareness, had escaped the night before, on account of the gun. As Ziza-Hybrid, she also knew it would be treason to destroy the Titinha, or even to consider destroying her, the great leader of the Tititri. But it must be done if the masses of their people were to survive. The Titinha's plan would not allow any of their people to survive except the Titinha herself. And whoever her protector partner chose for her lieutenants. Where did that leave the rest of the people? For instance, the Ziza-Hybrid?

Now Ziza within the Hybrid understood where the mud blocked feet were taking them. They were following the Titinha. As was the other Hybrid who followed them, the one who pattered like a panther. Together, they would have to commit treason and destroy their leader. The Titinha lodged within the human child, not within the mother. Ziza's people almost had her the night before, the night of the gun, which forced the parasite within Ziza to flower into the Ziza-Hybrid. This they knew, now that their conversion was complete:

The Titinha would not escape again.

CHAPTER EIGHTEEN

MIST DESCENDED OVER THE mountaintops, sweeping down the sides of the mountains, swallowing the padded shape of the diminutive guide ahead of Landon. He struggled to keep up. The guide might be small, but his step was swift and sure.

Landon's goggles fogged up, and icy prickles tingled against the strip of exposed flesh between his bandana and the goggles. Molly whimpered in the child carrier strapped to his back. He wondered if it was really his daughter complaining about the cold wind that freeze-dried flesh, or if it was the alien within her.

He didn't expect to be out here already. Shortly after his encounter with the warden, Doctor Chan had informed him that the guide who would take him to the goatherder was awaiting him at the prison gate. Taking action, Landon decided, was better than arguing with Warden Hermanson about joining the rescue mission. As far as he knew, Hermanson's group hadn't even assembled yet.

Besides, finding the goatherder, letting him do his magic on Molly, could eliminate his need for Summer to help him. *If*, that is, if his magic worked. It was a long shot, but he was running out of options.

The uneven terrain of the ravine, along with the additional

weight of Molly on his back, brought irregular tweaks of pain to his shoulder. He moved cautiously, struggling to maintain his balance. Loose rocks ranged in size from pebbles to stepping stones, and they rolled and slipped beneath his feet, threatening to trip him. Now that they'd left the prison far below, his lungs felt cleansed raw from sucking in the moist air, which also brought a taste of sea air. The throbs racing up and down his body settled into a welcome numbness.

He scanned the gloom ahead, searching for movement that would indicate Summer's band of prisoners heading this way, returning down the mountain to the prison. He wondered if he should just hijack her if they crossed paths, but he supposed such an action would violate procedure. Landon had always been a by-the-book sort of man. Not so much, today.

If he intercepted Summer, and *if* she cooperated, then he might not even need Chan's goatherder. Finding him out here in this endless ruggedness seemed an impossible task, but the guide Chan had hooked him up with seemed capable. His name was Aquilino, which he said in his broken English meant Eagle. Landon wondered if it was a nickname for his eyesight. Or maybe his agility. Or size. He was only about twice the size of Molly, but he moved with the sureness of knowing exactly where to find the solitary man, alone with his goats in all these mountains.

Landon grunted and steadied his breathing, attention alert. He listened intently for the sounds, tamped and muted by the misty fog, of murmuring voices or the thud of footfalls or the scrabble of sliding rocks to indicate a troop of people descending the ravine ahead, but he heard nothing beyond his own circle of clumsiness. Not even the soft plodding of his own guide's footsteps. Nor the distant cries of a gull, brought in with the advancing seas.

Molly squealed, imitating the seagulls. He shivered, wondering if the alien within her was communicating in gull-talk. The lone bird they'd seen soaring the prison walls as they prepared to leave on this trek had distracted Molly while he wrestled her into a prison-issue wind jacket and face mask. The smallest size blanketed her, and he wrapped the extra folds around her legs and feet, tucking them inside the child carrier. He wondered why Greer hadn't protested about his bringing Molly outside. His sister almost seemed delighted for the reprieve from childcare. As if she had something else planned.

And so Landon, Molly, and the little guide had set out from the prison, listening to the cries of that lone gull. Now, he heard nothing except the deep breathing of Molly, sleeping nestled against the back of his neck, and his own abrasive sounds as he set off spinning, tumbling rocks.

Nothingness filled him with a sense of emptiness.

Like the void that had filled him after Summer.

It had been a long but sure and steady road for Summer, getting here, to these Patagonian mountains where the ultimate prison lodged, isolated. She should've seen it coming. There was nothing he could've done to save her from the fate she'd chosen for herself.

He sighed with regret for all the losses. His, as well as Summer's.

Now she would spend the rest of her life here in Patagonia, with soaring mountains like the Rockies of her origins. Except here, water lapped at their base. She'd done a lot of spinning in her life, but she hadn't escaped who she really was. If only

Landon had seen that sooner. If only he'd been able to read her mind.

A shrill cry slid down the slope to his right, jolting him from his memories. He jerked to the right, following the sound. Ice bullets sprayed and stung the flesh of his cheek.

"Wait," he called to Aquilino as he froze in his tracks to listen. It was a voice he'd heard. Molly's masked cheek pulled away from his neck, and her body stiffened against his back.

The wind wailed and slammed against him like a wall of ice. He staggered backwards and blinked, although goggles protected his eyes.

Aquilino materialized out of the gloom before him. "No much farther," he shouted, gesturing up the ravine. His arms, padded and buffered inside his wind suit, seemed to puff out to deflect the wind.

Landon had heard the wind, he realized, not a voice. He sighed and trudged on. Molly relaxed against his back.

He worked his way up the slope of the ravine, following the guide's shape, but he saw Titan again, in his memory. H.F. had sent him on the mission to Titan to test his tachcom from that vast distance. In his mind now, he saw those towers, stair-stepping against the backdrop of the ice cavern. Alien-made, abandoned towers. He and the others on that mission had been unable to penetrate the towers. The mission was scarcely able to escape the cavern with their lives intact.

Landon suspected that the trouble with Summer went back even farther than that mission.

Settling those troubles, tying up loose ends with her, was the surface reason why he'd had to come to Patagonia. And once they finally reconnected, Molly probably wouldn't even remember her mother. It had been half her lifetime ago when she'd last seen her mother, being hauled away by the authorities after the bombing incident on SpaceHab. Thankfully, the bomb hadn't gone off, and even if it had, it wouldn't have been powerful enough to rupture the outer hull of the wheel. But it had still done plenty of damage, even if the plot had fizzled. The failed bomb had completely destroyed his marriage.

But the real reason why he was hauling Molly up the side of these Patagonian mountains went far deeper. Deeper than finding a goatherder to interfere with Molly's tracking chip. He had to go to the root of the problem and force Summer to release the alien from Molly. She could do that, he felt certain. Summer had some sort of relationship with the Tititri. All along, he'd thought it was the Savers who'd brainwashed Summer, but now he was certain it was really the Tititri. He'd been blind to Summer's involvement with the aliens.

He'd been blind to a lot of things.

Now he saw things clearer, even though mist enveloped him.

The ravine finally opened onto an alpine meadow. By now, his legs had gone numb, too. He paused at the lip of the meadow, where grasses were already dying back from approaching winter. Aquilino charged on, following a narrow animal track through bristly foliage, scrubby as it was. On the other side of the meadow he could barely make out the shape of another rise in the endless chain of rises that composed these mountains.

Endless.

He smelled the goats before he saw any hut. He smelled their wet, fecal-matted wool, and then he spied the goat pens, fenced with wire. Behind the goats' twitching tails, a small, turf-covered shed wedged into a crevice at the base of twin peaks. Goats pressed their snouts into the hexagonal openings between the wires of the fence and bleated, sounding like a pitiful laugh. Their sharp little heads turned, and their impatient eyes glimmered, following Landon's passage toward the hut.

The hut tucked into a fold in the mountain's side. Stones built up its foundations and grasses thatched its roof, allowing the hut to blend into its surroundings. Piles of plant debris — leaves, twigs, bark, and the like — heaped around the perimeter. Landon wouldn't have spotted the hut at all if not for Aquilino's pointing it out. And the smell of the goats.

He kicked off a mini-avalanche of loose rock, a residue of crumbles from the giant granite peaks that speared the limits of the breathable atmosphere. The heavy cleats of his boots dragged at his ankles, twisting them with each roll of the rocks. Splinters of pain ricocheted up through his knees, joining the strain of Molly's weight on his back, knifing open the rip in his shoulder. His nose tickled from the splatters of mud droplets he was kicking up in his haste to follow the guide.

Aquilino strode to the door of the hut and cracked it open. Rosy light leaked out from behind the creaking door of sticks. Landon moved forward, feeling himself steered into the light. His flesh crawled.

A warm fire smoldered in the hearth just beyond his reach.

He stepped inside the hut and glanced around, but he didn't see any human caretaker of the goats. There was no one here who could help him.

CHAPTER NINETEEN

GOOD.

Now she was free, Greer thought as the door of her guestroom closed behind Landon and Molly, leaving her alone. She waited, listening to the footsteps of her brother and the babbling sounds of his daughter fade away down the hall, and then she waited some more. It would only be a little while that they were gone. She couldn't wait too long to make her move.

Finally, she opened the door and poked her head out into the hall. No one was in sight on this upper level. A wall of windows showed her the mountains surrounding this facility.

Not that Molly was a burden to her. Although, taking care of a little girl had certainly turned Greer's life upside down. A gal needed a break every once in a while. A gal needed to be a gal sometimes, and not just a surrogate mother.

Greer tiptoed across the noiseless, vinyl surface of the hall floor and touched her nose to the cold slickness of the glass wall of windows. Far below, two miniature figures materialized out of the gray gloom as little more than dots from this distance. One of them, she could tell from the baby on his back, was Landon. The other figure must be the escort that the warden guy had insisted must always accompany a visitor on these grounds. She didn't think it was the warden himself. The escort looked too little, as compared to her brother.

They were moving away from the prison, following some sort of path along a ridge into the mountains.

The mountains? Why on earth were the seagulls luring them *up there*? Regret burned through Greer like acid indigestion. Regret, intertwined with doubt. Maybe she shouldn't have allowed Landon to take Molly outside, not even for a short innocent outing to see the birds. That's what he'd said they were doing.

Even so, Molly would enjoy a little special time with her daddy. It would only be a short hike outside, and besides, hiking would take them closer to the seagulls Molly had befriended. And anyway, they'd probably return before Greer could accomplish her mission.

She'd better hurry.

She had taken on such a frenzy over that room with the body drawers, that now she had to see it through. She *had* to. Besides, she had to prove to everyone that she was not stupid. She could tell that something about that room with body drawers and kaleidoscope monitors had spoken to Molly. Something had pulled the little girl there. Something had reacted to Molly's presence by shutting everything off. Greer had to find out what that special something was, if she was to take care of her niece properly. And she sure as heck couldn't find out anything if Molly was with her. She would find out what, and then she would tell Landon all about it when he came back from his little outing in another hour or so, and then he would have no choice but to view his sister with new respect. Yes. That was the plan.

She pulled away from the window and rubbed the smudge her breath had left there, leaving a swirling smear. Oh well.

There was enough daylight trickling in through the gloom of cloud cover to masque her prints. She tiptoed down the hall in the general direction of the medical facility. She took care not to step on any cracks where sensors might lodge. She didn't want to squeak the floor, not knowing who might hear her from behind the closed doors she sped past. There must be a stairwell along here that would take her down to the basement level and all those tunnels where non-prisoners could move from wing to wing without the observant eyes of the guards tracking their every move from their guard towers. She moved on in silence.

New respect would gain her... What? Well, she didn't know, not exactly. After all, she already had legal guardianship of the baby. What more did she need?

She needed her brother to stop needling her, to stop harassing her about her incompetence.

There. That door dead ahead looked like a door into a stairwell. It had a cold, steel look, with a little window pane up so high you couldn't see through it. It had a steel handle. It definitely wasn't a door into someone's quarters.

She wrapped her fingers around the handle, held her breath, and squeezed, pushing against the door. It opened into a rounded shaft that smelled of wet cement. To her surprise, a smart pole — or at least, she hoped it was smart — plunged down into the center of the shaft. She grabbed hold, the way that crazy reporter woman had shown her — only yesterday? The pole grabbed back, and she slid down into its shaft, down, down, down.

Wheeee...

If she weren't so terrified, this could be fun.

Terrified? There was no reason for her to be terrified, not

in the care of technology, which couldn't fail her. Besides, she owned her surroundings. She had every business to be here. If the warden guy had been more forthright with her, she wouldn't have had to find this smart pole on her own.

And it was gentle. Dank, basement air lifted up to her face and fluffed the wisps of her hair tails from the sweaty back of her neck.

She felt herself slowing. The pole must be coming to the end of her thrill ride. Darn. Her toes touched the landing pad at the bottom of a pit and the pole unclasped her. She took a breath and stepped away, stumbling with the return to her own mobility. Another square of a window slightly above her head indicated the presence of a door, and she leaned against its steel bulk. The wall cracked open and she tripped through, out into the dungeon-like corridor that connected the guards' residential sector to the medical facility where Chan the woman doctor experimented on alien beings and Brant the tough warden guy protected her secret.

Greer would soon expose them, and then Landie would thank her. He would appreciate the trouble she was going to and consider her with new admiration.

Landon, she meant.

Greer was accustomed to being admired.

She tiptoed on, expecting one of those mechanical spiders to creep out of a wall crevice at any moment, alerting her presence to the warden guy. What would he do to her then? A thrill coursed through her, imagining the rough feel of his hands manhandling her, wrestling her against a wall, breathing heavily into her face.

The thrill drained away when she reminded herself of his

irritating lack of manners.

She sped on.

Found another stairwell. This one with old-fashioned steps. She huffed and climbed. Round and round.

Dizzy, she paused on a landing to catch her breath, and then pushed her way through a door. She found herself in the clinical hall where she'd waited with Molly. She retraced the steps they'd taken earlier when Molly pretended to be a bird, flying down the hall to that open door that had gotten them in so much trouble.

The door was closed now. She leaned close, placing her ear against its slick surface, as if she could hear what went on inside the door or on the other side of the door. If this place had smart poles for fast escapes, why couldn't it have smart doors, too?

With her hands, she smoothed her fingers across the polished surface until her fingers detected miniscule ridges that ran like veins through the door. Ah. Here was the weakness. She pressed her ear against one of the ridges and listened.

Someone was inside. She could hear footsteps, or rather, the footsteps reverberated within her being. She heard swishing sounds, or rather, swishes pulsed through her. She felt the warmth of someone's nearby presence.

And then the door swung inward, pulling her off balance. She tumbled into the room, eye level to a pair of manly legs with sexy protrusions — kneecaps — under the stiff cloth of charcoal gray slacks.

"Something you are looking for, Ms. Cameron?" Brant the warden guy said, towering above her.

She held out her hand, so that he could help haul her upright, but he didn't take it. She clambered up to her feet and thrust her chin up, but still she couldn't look him evenly in the eye. "Um, yes. I lost an earring. It must be here somewhere."

"Come in, and let us look for it." He swung the door wide, inviting her into the room with body drawers and machines, burping again.

If he was so willing to admit her, she wasn't so sure she wanted to go inside after all. But she couldn't very well extricate herself from the situation now that she'd made it up. So she followed him into the cold air of the room that twanged and hummed and clicked and smelled faintly of... Chemicals? That's what the woman doctor had said. They stored dangerous chemicals in here.

But no. It wasn't a chemical smell but more of a... She didn't know what. It almost smelled like Aunt Jewel's kitchen when the dear sweet lady had been baking... Cardamon bread. Yes!

Maybe the drawers Greer had thought were body drawers were really ovens. But if the warden was baking bread, then shouldn't the air feel warm in here? And why a dozen ovens?

"What does it look like?" Brant said, closing the door behind him with a soft click of the latch.

"What does *what* look like?"

"Your earring." The twist of his lips, as if he'd tasted a sour lemon, told her that he didn't believe her story.

"Oh! Um..." Her index finger darted to her bare earlobe. "It's a pearl. It could've rolled anywhere, under any of those machines, for instance." She waved her arm to indicate the array of flashing screens. If he was going to lock her in here, then she would have to prove to him that he couldn't frighten her. She sashayed closer to the equipment, making a deliberate show of examining the patterns of colorful lines and squiggles. One of the screens showed what looked like the inside of a room, filled with moving parts that spun round and round. She almost felt dizzy watching the cubes and spheres spin.

He touched her elbow and she nearly jumped out of her skin. "It would be on the floor, would it not?"

"Oh! Why, yes, of course. I just couldn't help but admire these interesting patterns on your displays. And all the lights, oh my! What does all this stuff do?"

"Nothing that would interest you."

"That's what Landon always thinks, too. But he's usually wrong. About me, that is. About what interests me."

"Trust me, what goes on here is of no interest to you."

"But see, that's where you're wrong." And besides, why should she trust *him*?

He chuckled softly, diabolically. "I am paid to never be wrong."

His tone of voice, like the villain in an old-time movie, made the hairs on the back of her neck stand rigid. Her spine stiffened. She eyeballed the door, but he stood between it and her. She laughed it off, flicking her wrist. "Oh yeah? What are you going to do about it? Shoot me?"

"Only if I have to. I suggest you either find your earring or return to your quarters. Shall I summon an escort now?"

"Only if he's cute. And if he takes me someplace interesting, like the one you called for Landon."

The warden's neck snapped sideways. "What are you talking about?"

"You sent someone to take Landon and Molly outside to see the seagulls."

His eyes narrowed.

"Didn't you?"

Still, he did not answer.

She went on. "Well, someone did. Molly is so taken with those seagulls. What's with them, anyway? They almost seem tame. Do you do experiments on them, too?"

"Those goddamned birds are a filthy nuisance. The kid's mother makes it worse. The kid must have inherited the same talent."

A chill tickled Greer's spine. He was wrong. It wasn't talent, not exactly. It was more like *ability*. Now she understood. The aliens spoke to Molly *and* Summer through the *birds*.

CHAPTER TWENTY

SUMMER TUMBLED IN A HEAP onto what felt like a spongy floor.

The faint gloom of the outdoors trickled in through the hole Summer had breached far above her head. Ghostly lighting pooled around the heap of her body like a fading spotlight. "Diamond? Where are you?"

As her eyes gradually adjusted to the dark, she realized Diamond wasn't with her. He must still be outside. Inside, shadowy shapes of rectangles and ovoids emerged just beyond her reach. In this pool of faint light where she lay, warm air embraced her skin. Chemical-organic smells seeped into her lungs, tingling their way through her body with thawing warmth.

Outside, voices snarled and jumbled together, piling on top of each other, mounting in an angry crescendo. It sounded as if the guards had caught up to Diamond, restraining him. He'd sacrificed himself, as had Amazon.

She crawled onto her good knee, pushed with her palms against the soft, squishy floor, and rose unsteadily to her feet. *Must help Diamond!* She wobbled — no, it was the dark space around her that tilted — as she lost her balance and fell sideways.

Plunging, rolling...

The voices outside and above screamed in unison, their

sound dropping away. From their dopplered howl, she understood in a flash that the glacier had shifted again, spitting the guards off its edge and tossing them down into the canyon far below.

She remained safe here inside. The chemical air around her trembled and rattled and shook, buffering her as forces flung her against one shadowy shape after another.

One last thundering boom exploded, and then silence.

Stillness.

Darkness.

The trickle of gloom from the hole she'd entered was gone. The hole, or door, had sealed shut behind her, trapping her inside some kind of burrow far underground.

Safe.

* * * * *

Summer awoke in darkness, feeling calm. Soothed. A pleasant smell wafted around her, one that she could not quite place. It reminded her of home, of beeswax and lemon.

She did not remember having fallen asleep. She did not know why she'd awakened in the dark. Nor did she know where she was, except not on her cot in her prison cell. She uncurled from her prone position and reached across the spongy surface of thick foam where she lay, but she felt no edge.

She'd slept on a floor.

Then she remembered falling, the long plunge through a slick tunnel. Diamond had pushed her into an opening in the metal contraption that looked like a hollow tree trunk half-buried under glacier. It had been a chute, dropping her into this dark place with the padded floor. And then it had shifted, tunneling her farther underground. She pushed herself up to her feet, staggering a bit under the weight of her disorientation.

She did not think she was blind. She could not see well, that's all. There was a difference between not seeing and blindness. Shapes resolved slowly in the murky haze of the dark.

She turned slowly, taking in the murk. Tall, skinny shapes, like upright spears fencing her into a circle, pumped up and down as she turned, constantly shifting into new shapes and patterns. She felt as if she were an insignificant, tiny speck inside a giant gear, and she watched the gear's teeth cycle and gnash around her.

Tinkling laughter echoed in her head. Someone... some *thing* had invaded her thoughts and seemed to enjoy reading her state of confusion.

Summer's mind roiled with the residue of her life's failures, her losses, her sacrifices, and all for what?

All for *this*.

The floor shifted beneath her feet, rocking her as pain rocketed up her legs.

"Diamond! Where the hell are you?" He'd brought her here, to this place with the spongy floor. He should be here, somewhere. Then she remembered their escape from the guards, their whips, their rifles, and — "*Amazon!*" A weight crushed her heart, dragging her down to her knees.

She needed them. Her friends.

But she did not have friends. Had not had friends, not real friends, not since...

Need. *Need!* "Need" was a word Summer had discarded long ago, she couldn't remember when. Had it been... All the way back to the life she used to lead in Colorado? Her life before Landon.

Ever since Landon, she had been functioning on automatic. Others had controlled her destiny. She no longer questioned why she ended up in the places she ended up. There was a larger plan for her. The Savers had caught her up in their spider web. The moon voice was the spider. She did not flinch at the comparison. Yes, the moon voice was her friend. It had always soothed her during all her troubling times. It was the moon who had brought her into this dark place. And yet...

She did not feel that the laughter in her head belonged to any friend.

Everything that had gone before in her life, ceased to exist. Because now and here were all that existed. Everything she had ever done before had been for the purpose of bringing her here to this dark destination. She had succeeded. She was finished, her journey finished, a costly journey. The child she'd had to create. And then lose. It was all for this.

She collapsed the rest of the way to the spongy floor and shuddered with useless sobs. Everything, done.

A new smell invaded her darkness, making her aware of another's presence. She lifted her head, touching her cheeks to the newcomer's smell, a combination of rotting fecal matter and the zesty tang of freshly cut herbs. Then from the darkness came a soft rattling sound, the way aspen leaves shimmered in a breeze. Finally, something cool kissed the top of her head, caressed down the side of her face and throat, in much the same way she had stroked her baby, before...

Before joining the cause against aliens had thrown away her former life.

Summer jerked upright, stumbling, staggering, tripping as she hauled herself up onto her feet. Tweaks of pain stabbed through her with each twist and turn. Her gaze burned through the murk and connected onto a shadowy figure of a — human? — who stood before her. A tall figure, towering a head taller than her, it was draped in ropes, reminding her of a gangly tree entangled with sucker vines.

"We have been waiting for you," the vine-wrapped figure said in a purring, male voice. It was a familiar voice, but Summer couldn't remember who the voice belonged to.

"Who are you?" Summer said, and as soon as she spoke the words, a wave of understanding crushed her. He was the shaman who sometimes came to the prison, trying to exorcise the Savers out of the prisoners' being.

"They call me El Pastor. Do not fear."

She flinched and shrank backwards a step. The Asses must have sent him here. The ropes looping around him, forming his cape, must be the torturers' whips. "Diamond," she mumbled. Diamond had set her up for this. Diamond...not a friend at all, but a betrayer. All along, Diamond had known exactly where to bring her. To this.

Why?

"We are here to help you," El Pastor said.

That's more or less what the Asses said at the prison, too, but she did not believe that for a minute. No one wanted to help her. Not ever. Because they thought she was crazy.

When she wasn't, not in reality.

In reality, she could have been the savior of Earth. If only they would let her do her work, instead of locking her away. "Help me how?"

"Fulfill your purpose."

"My purpose is dead. I can't do anything now to help the cause. Aliens are going to invade." She could tell this to El Pastor because he was the only one she'd ever met since the Savers had recruited her who did not assume she was crazy. "What can we do anymore, with most of us locked up? Diamond tried to set us loose, but he failed. It's too late now."

"No," El Pastor said. "It is not too late."

She scoffed. "How would you know? The aliens even hijacked the implants the Savers gave me. That's how they talked to me. They are already on their way here, to take over our world. Not even the Savers can stop them now."

"No." His voice dropped to a whisper.

Shadowy shapes cycled around them, vibrating the cavern with a soft rumble. The sponge of the floor hummed, sending tickles creeping up through the bones of her feet.

"Where is Diamond?" Summer felt dread ripple upwards through her. "Who are you, really, that you think anything different?"

El Pastor's shadowy shape shifted in the dark. He was apparently tipping his head back, looking up into the darkness above their heads. His body swayed in time with the churning gears. Soft, ululating sounds spilled from him. "...Teee...teee...treee..."

But it wasn't his voice that raised to a new level of pitch. It was the voice of a woman, the same woman who'd spoken before.

Summer touched her ears, but it was too late. Her implants were already hijacked. She'd thought it was the moon voice speaking to her, but all along, she was wrong. And now the alien had caught her. In its spider's web.

CHAPTER TWENTY-ONE

THE SMOKY WARMTH OF THE fireplace drew Landon farther inside the hut. If the goatherder had abandoned his fire, then he couldn't have gone far away, not for long. Granted, the flames smoldered rather than flared inside the stone-lined hearth. It was difficult to know how long the tender of the fire had been away.

"You know where else he might be?" Landon said, turning to look at Aquilino, who waited silently in the open doorway.

"El Pastor?" The guide scanned the rugged landscape beyond the hut, as if he could see into the clouds or fog that swathed the peaks surrounding them like a jagged jawline of broken teeth.

"Who else?"

"No far."

"We might as well wait for him inside," Landon said. "Come in and shut the door." Such as it was. The door looked like a row of branches tied together and sealed with twining tufts of turf. Probably it was medicinal leaves and roots, Landon thought with a snort, selected to repel unwanted guests.

It hadn't worked.

The heavy, organic smell of the smoke made him suspect the fire was fueled by something earthy and local. The goatherder probably burned peat, and if so, the fire could've been smoldering like this for a long time. Something had pulled him away. Another house call, perhaps. He must have clients other than the prison.

Landon would make himself at home while he waited. He nodded at Aquilino, who hesitantly followed Landon inside and shut the door behind him with a creak of its weathered sticks.

Landon pushed his goggles off his face, unwrapped his scarves and slid the child carrier from his back. Molly stirred while he maneuvered her from the carrier and murmured "prrrriiii," blowing bubbles of saliva. He laid her down on El Pastor's bed of goat hides, where she snuggled into their fur, turning her nose as if to inhale their musk, and then fell back to sleep. For an instant, a new worry prickled him. She slept too soundly. Almost as if she'd been drugged.

Impossible. He'd carried her with him for at least the last couple of hours, maybe more, ever since the midday meal... It could've happened there. Watching her, holding his breath, pushing his worries away, he quietly unsealed the front edge of his wind jacket.

When he was sure he hadn't awakened her, he deposited his gear onto an old-style plastic table, scarred and scratched with years of abuse. It sat like a showpiece in the middle of the narrow room, centered between the fire on one side and a square window on the other. A sheet of plastic covered the window, not much larger than a human head, and rattled and snapped erratically against the wind. Through the plastic he could make out the rectangular shape of the goats' shelter inside their pen.

Landon moved closer to the fire, holding his hands out before him to warm them. When Aquilino failed to join him, he glanced over his shoulder. The guide still stood unmoving behind him, just inside the door of sticks.

"You didn't expect him to be gone, did you?" Landon said, surveying the square room. Molly sighed in her sleep and rolled over. "He can't have left his goats long, so I imagine he'll be back soon."

"Depends." Aquilino shrugged and took a step, which put him half the distance from the door to the table. He stopped there, apparently reluctant to advance any farther.

Landon's stomach rumbled, twisting with unease. It wasn't only Molly who worried him... He glanced over at the sleeping child and back to Aquilino. The guide still hadn't taken off his jacket. As if he sensed some unseen danger. He was the eagle, after all. He'd spotted something. Landon suddenly felt vulnerable, separated from Molly, stripped of his gear. If they had to vacate this place all of a sudden, as El Pastor must've done, Landon wouldn't be ready.

He hated not being ready. Even more, he hated being vulnerable.

"Depends on what?" he asked Aquilino.

"Who needs him."

"But you said he hadn't gone very far. Sounds like you know his habits pretty well."

"I don' know him." The tartan plaid scarf that wrapped Aquilino's throat slipped from its knot. One fringed end dangled loose.

"You know him well enough that you know where he lives."

"Sure, I come here a few times." The guide scowled. Apparently, he didn't enjoy coming here. "Bring messages from Doctor Chan. She wants him to have one of these." He pulled a palm-sized device from his pocket and showed it to Landon. It looked like a mini sat-link. Battery operated, he presumed. He'd seen no generator up here, nor heard its rumble.

"Not a bad idea for such a remote place as this," Landon said. "I take it, he refused?"

Aquilino nodded. "El Pastor says he already knows when Doctor Chan wants him to come to prison. He don' need this talk machine." He slipped the link back into his pocket, lifted his goggles and contemplated Molly. A moonbeam streamed through the square window and caught her face as if a spotlight shone on her while she slept.

"But he didn't know this time, did he?" Landon said. "He didn't know that someone from the prison needed him."

"Maybe because is you and not Doctor Chan."

"Same difference. Chan recommended him to me. If this goatherder claims he knows when Chan summons him, then he should've known this time, too. But he didn't, not if he left. You think that's deliberate? Or did something change?"

"Maybe he on his way to the prison now, and we miss him."

"Is there another way down?" As attentive as Landon had been on the way up, watching for Summer coming down, he would've spied someone else on the trail, even in the fog. And if he'd missed noticing, then eagle-eyed Aquilino wouldn't have. He was sure about that.

Aquilino shrugged. "He have other business. I do not know what. We wait."

Right. Landon grunted and paced the hard-packed dirt floor of the small room. Another delay.

Aquilino dug through baskets of supplies, rattling tin plates and cups, but still, Molly did not stir. He filled the cups with a urine yellow liquid — coca tea, he hoped, and plates with bread, and then motioned Landon to the fire with their food and drink.

They had nothing else to do but wait. Pacing got him nowhere. He sank down onto the goat hides and sipped the tea, which was about as appetizing as sucking on straw. Even so, it fortified him.

He settled in for the unknown wait. Night fell as they waited.

"Nice scarf," Landon finally said to break the stillness of their wait. He motioned at Aquilino's tartan plaid, which the guide still hadn't removed. Something Scottish seemed unlikely in a place like this. "Where'd you get it?"

"A gift," Aquilino said with a shrug.

Landon snorted. "I haven't seen any gift shops down here, much to my sister's dismay."

"No from shop. Sometimes visitors to prison leave their things behind and Doctor Chan, she give to me." The ends of Aquilino's mouth turned down in a scowl.

"That's a good deal for you. So you had a Scottish visitor at the prison?"

"No. Was scientist, like you, only he come with team of Executors, from headquarters. From Holland Annex."

Landon sat up from his relaxed slump. "You remember his name?"

"Van Pelt."

"Van Pelt was *here*?"

"Yes. You know him? Friend of Doctor Chan." Aquilino waggled his eyebrows.

Landon clattered his tin plate and cup, setting them down, and then he scrambled to his feet. Van Pelt was one of only a handful of theoretical researchers into tachyonic communication, and he had somehow ended up *here*, in Patagonia. Afterwards, he'd returned to the Holland Annex where he scribbled a note about the Tititri and then hanged himself.

But he hadn't finished writing his note.

Landon shivered and paced the hut. Someone else could've made it look as if Van Pelt had hanged himself. Because of what he'd learned about the aliens, something he'd learned *here*, Van Pelt had been silenced.

After his death, his techs finally revealed the data Van Pelt had been working on, an analysis of the tachyonic stream that H.F. thought was a message from aliens. Van Pelt read it as "Don't come."

Don't come *here*?

But Landon was already here, chasing another wild idea of H.F.'s, to find the alien outpost. Now he suspected the old man's fear wasn't so unfounded. Furthermore, he suspected the aliens were using Molly to get at Landon. To kill him, as they'd killed Van Pelt.

"Lannnnndon," said a woman's whispery soft voice from the shadows filling the corners of the room.

The back of his neck tingled as he whirled around. A goat hide slipped from the bed, and then Molly dropped to the floor. She toddled a few steps toward him, into the circle of light flickering from the fireplace. Her eyes glowed green, an unnatural shade like glittering emeralds, the same way he'd seen them change before. Now, as before, the baby's facial features shifted proportion, and the alien woman surfaced from within Molly's face.

"It is time," the woman said through Molly. She — it —

sighed, echoing whatever ancient knowledge she'd garnered across light years of space and time.

Aquilino gasped, muttered a few words in his native language, and crossed himself.

Landon stepped closer to the being who used the body of his daughter. Molly's essence seemed to have submerged somewhere within her toddler's two-foot tall frame. "Time for what?"

"To go to my people."

"Who are you? *What* are you?" He had a right to know, if the alien wanted to kill him.

"I am the Titinha, keeper of the Tititri, of the world Ti."

Landon felt as if his blood simultaneously froze and boiled. He stood face to face with the alien who'd taken possession of his daughter, and he couldn't think how to get Molly back. He felt frozen in place with helpless fury. "What have you done with my daughter? Leave her the hell alone!"

"Your daughter will be well cared for. PRI watches over us."

"Let Molly go!"

"Have no fear. I will release her when we are done."

"You'll let her go NOW!" He lunged at Molly's body, occupied by the Titinha, cared for by PRI, whatever in hell that was.

She — it — twisted to one side and darted away with a speed he'd not seen Molly ever use. The alien being drove Molly's body to the door of twigs, yanked it open, and disappeared into the night outside.

CHAPTER TWENTY-TWO

ZIZA FONSECA'S BODY SUITED the Tititri well. It was a lithe, conditioned body, well adapted to running, to plunging through the plant sea. Her appendages festered with sores and propelled her through this foreign, liquid-air place. A warm wetness slicked across the outer layer of the body of the jungle woman.

We call it 'skin', Ziza whispered from inside the parasite's nest. She had switched places with the parasite that had ridden her up until now.

The essence of the original known as Ziza Fonseca lodged deep within the hardened body of this indigenous lifeform. The original stirred, feeding information to the Tititri, and together they blended their knowledge as one, thinking of itself as Ziza-Hybrid. Only with such blending could they survive in their new home.

Ziza-Hybrid assimilated the new information exploding from within and around her. A shade of light that she had never seen before on Ti blazed through the surrounding air. She felt both blinded and smothered in this land. Her new world.

Jungle, the original reminded the Tititri with a tickle of their mind.

"Jun-gle," Ziza-Hybrid said, trying out the word through

her human mouth.

She had never seen a single leaf before, although the ancestors had passed down many stories about leaf-covered plants. And vast seas, too. Not even the ancestors could have imagined the existence of such countless numbers of plants as what filled jungle, so many that they pressed together, forming a sea. She drowned in the sea of plants.

Humans had already adapted to this wet world. Why should the Tititri not use the human skins? It seemed a more promising mode of survival than the Titinha's plan to grow new bodies for the masses.

As it was, her already adapted lungs labored to sponge in the abundant oxygen.

Mãe's moonrose vine, Ziza the original thought.

"Moon?" Ziza-Hybrid glanced up at the ceiling of leaves, searching for an opening that would reveal this wet world's moon. It was an eye watching over Tititri in the name of survival. The PRI, the machine that served as the Titinha's protector partner, had been sent to this world's moon long ago, according to the stories the ancestors had sung about the crisis of Ti.

But she saw no moon. No glimmer of its light shimmering against the unknown color of jungle. Here, the air dripped a color between leaves that did not fall within the range of reds she'd known on Ti. She had never seen such colored air before.

Green, Ziza whispered in their new, blended mind.

With the knowledge of Ziza seeping through her, Ziza-Hybrid inhaled deeply, exploring the air tang with her confiscated set of breathing lungs and accessories. She leaned into the greenness, letting its slick surfaces wash over her throbbing, pulsing exterior.

No moon meant that her blueprint sent from Ti had escaped PRI's interference. PRI could not touch her, not now.

And she was alive!

We survive!

Her life wasn't only about escape, not as the original had believed before. Now that she had flowered into Ziza-Hybrid she understood more clearly. It was about survival. The Mundomba, the original's mother's people, had known all about survival here in the jungle. Mãe had been right all along, and Ziza the failure. Ziza-Hybrid would redeem her.

We rush to where? The original still felt her old worries.

The Tititri who now drove the original's body confessed to some worries, too, but they were long ago and far away, on Ti, when she and the other dissidents had stolen the blueprint-maker. How would it convert her? How would it send her through space on her journey to this single-star system? What if PRI had read the data wrong? Would she die as a blueprint, or would her blueprint land on a host who could not serve her?

She had let the other dissidents talk herself out of her doubts. All of them would be reborn again, they promised, when implanted on indigenous lifeforms, whose skins would carry both Tititri and the original. Otherwise, what difference would it make how she died? On Ti they were going to die anyway.

Death is rebirth in the jungle.

The green air screeched with sounds, as if warning of intruders. Ziza-Hybrid paused the movement of her original's appendages and scanned the green-ness around her. Leaves shifted and shadows swayed, swinging and swooping, matching the direction of her course to the jumping place. Her pulse hammered and squished through her skin, an echo of the intruders.

Monkeys, the original explained.

"Mon-keys?" The hammering slowed to a tickle. Not the Xyvors, then. She exhaled warm, wet air. The original's appendages weakened their support, and she collapsed to a cool slick of fallen leaves.

Then, the Xyvors had not found the Tititri after all. She and the others would be safe here, hiding out on this world called green.

Safe.

But not completely. Not yet. Not until she released the masses of Tititri blueprints, imprisoned by PRI. That meant she would have to commit treason and stop their leader, the Titinha. The only way to stop her would be to kill the indigenous lifeform that hosted the Titinha, a being known as Summer Jeunne-Walker.

Not Summer. Molly! The original screamed in her mind, searing it with distress.

"Mol-ly?"

Killing would make Ziza-Hybrid no better than the Xyvors. But it must be done. To ensure survival. Her blueprint knew the way to the jumping place. Guiding, gliding, the original's ill-formed feet pushed her upright and moved on, carrying her closer to fulfilling the hopes of the Tititri.

CHAPTER TWENTY-THREE

LANDON FROZE, ROOTED TO THE dirt floor of the goatherder's hut. Time froze. His world collapsed around him in agonizing slow motion as he watched his daughter run out into the Patagonian night. A single heartbeat later, he sprang after her.

"Molly!" he shouted.

Something snagged him, pulling him back into the hut. He snarled, turning to see what had caught him. Aquilino. "Zsssst," the guide said.

Landon shook him off. "She can't go out there by herself! She's just a baby."

"Not her they want," Aquilino said. "The bad ones, they want you."

"How would you know that?"

Aquilino tapped his temple with his index finger. "The goats tell me. I am the eagle."

A goat whisperer. He ignored that. "You know where they want her to go?"

"They leave us alone if they think you are no here."

"Look, we've got to stop her. There's no time to waste, man, don't you understand?"

Aquilino wagged his head. "No. I don' understand. How

El Pastor talk through little girl? But I trust him. He keep her safe from bad ones. You let him do what he must do, and you no make noise to bring bad ones here."

"No, you've got it wrong. That wasn't El Pastor talking just now. That was..." He thought more about it. Hell, maybe El Pastor *was* the alien. But the voice speaking through Molly had sounded like a woman's.

"You no know El Pastor like I know." Aquilino grabbed Landon's elbow. "You no understand our language, but you hear him too, yes?"

"It wasn't a 'he' speaking," Landon said, twisting out of the guide's grip. "It was a she. She called herself *the* Titinha."

As if that was a title, not a name. Keeper, she called herself. The keeper of the Tititri, her people. Came from the world Ti. Something called "PRI" watched over them. Some sort of protector, maybe the facilitator of their journey.

Time to go to them, she'd said. The Tititri were here.

Breaking away from the guide, Landon sprang once again for the door. Twigs creaked as the door flapped open in the breeze. Goats bleated, trying to tell him what they'd sensed. A predator, maybe. Aquilino's "bad ones." A cougar? Night air slapped his face as if with ice-cold fingers. The sound of goat hooves tapping nearby against rock seemed to hammer into his heart.

Not a cougar. The predator was the Tititri, stalking the humans inside the hut.

He scanned the silvery darkness. The mist had dissolved. Moonlight faintly illuminated the jagged outline of peaks above his head, peaks so close they looked as if he could touch them. Slowly, as his eyes adjusted, he could make out the path that etched through a field of boulders, toward the goat meadow on the other side of the rock scree. No movement darted in and out of rocks.

Molly had run out here without a coat. Hypothermia would set in before long, outside in the cold, without protection. Behind him, the warm blanket of air radiating from the fireplace sucked away, into the night. As his world had done just now, losing his baby girl. His world had diminished to a feather of smoke curling up from the ashes of the peat fire. No smoldering flames.

They wanted *him*, Aquilino had said. Well, okay, they could have him. But only if they let Molly go.

Aquilino stood in the doorway, holding out the coats Landon had left piled on the plastic table. Apparently, the eagle could read minds, too.

"Thanks," Landon mumbled, grabbing them. He wouldn't be much use to Molly if he froze. He wrestled to find a sleeve to plunge his arm into. His blood chilled, numbing the pain of the wound to his shoulder. He did not understand why Aquilino had heard Molly speak with El Pastor's voice, when clearly it had been a woman's voice. But then, he remembered what the linguist had theorized in the jungle, only the night before: the alien within Molly spoke in whatever language the intended receiver would understand.

Shamans — whether they were jungle women or mountain goatherders — had apparently been chosen as useful assistants to the encroaching aliens, the Tititri. But that didn't explain why they'd also taken Molly. She was no shaman. Her baby-like innocence had made her a target.

More likely, because she was Summer's daughter.

Flapping sounds of an unlatched gate came from the goat pen tucked into the side of the mountain. Landon whirled around, following the sound. In two swift strides he plowed into the fence. Clasping its thin wire construction, he shook it with soft rattles while groping for the open gate.

Aquilino's callused hand clamped down onto Landon's fingers as he nudged beside him at the fence. He hissed again and held up one finger, motioning for silence. He tensed, listening.

What? Landon formed the question with his lips. If he knew who and where the "bad ones" were, then he could fight them.

Aquilino's gaze rolled toward the back wall of the hut, where the wind snapped at the sheet of plastic that covered the window.

But there was no space back there, not the way the hut wedged up against the side of the mountain. Unless there was a cave, and either Molly or the predator — or both — had crawled into it, sheltering from the wind. Landon wanted to ask about the cave, but the slightest out-of-place sound would disrupt whatever it was that Aquilino seemed to understand about the situation. He was the eagle, after all.

Aquilino nodded at the back of the hut and whispered close to his ear, "El Pastor want me to go." He made a move through the gate into the goat pen.

"No, Aquilino, not you. I'm the one who needs to go find her."

The guide turned to look back at Landon and hissed again. "Not you. You stay here. Wait for *bebé*. El Pastor take good care of her."

Landon clutched his sleeve and yanked. His voice rose in spite of himself. "If you know so much, you must know where she is. Why won't you tell me?"

Aquilino gazed back at him in the moonlight, tipping his face with a sigh of sadness. "Is secret, the place El Pastor guards, because is entrance to another place. Is a type of gate, but no like this one." He swung the gate with a squeak. "This one only lets you pass through fence. You hide now." Swiftly, he slipped into the pen and blended with the shadowy forms of the goats.

Hide? Like hell. Landon darted after him, trying to imitate Aquilino's stealthy movement. As he approached a goat, however, using it for cover, it bleated and jumped away, only drawing more attention to Landon's clumsy passage through the goat pen.

The hell with this. He sped on, closing the distance to Aquilino, while the goats stirred and frisked and cried, announcing his presence to anyone — to any*thing* — who might be watching.

A secret gate. To another place. A gate to where?

In the moonlight, he could see the guide probing around the rocks at the base of the hut, under the window.

Moonlight.

The silvery beams had touched Molly while she slept on the bed of goat hides and seemed to nudge her awake. Landon stopped, turning to look up at the moon, flickering in and out from behind wispy clouds. Maybe *that* was where the Tititri hid. Up there on the Moon. He wondered if the "secret gate" was their method of transport between Earth and Moon. At any rate, the Tititri could be communicating with Molly, controlling her, via some sort of broadcast from the Moon.

As quickly as the idea came to him, he discarded it. The space agency would've picked up any such stealthy movement between here and there, or a broadcast long before now.

Aquilino crouched ahead and motioned at Landon to stay back and get down. Landon ducked and crabwalked closer.

His own lab on SpaceHab might've picked up any broadcast activity from the Moon. Why hadn't he?

Maybe his work up there on the space station explained all this. Aquilino claimed they wanted *him*, and now he wondered if it was on account of his tachyonic communication device. The Tititri must want to stop him from further work, from refining his tachcom.

But why?

In any case, the Tititri were biding their time, surfacing now and again to remind the humans of their presence. They hadn't gone away. One of them controlled his daughter, but Landon didn't think Molly was their real target. The aliens probably wanted to get at *him*, through Molly. They used Molly as a lure. Perhaps the aliens wanted him because they'd failed to get Van Pelt. He'd killed himself first.

The knowledge of the alien presence had apparently been too much for Van Pelt to handle, and he'd chosen death as the only way out. Death had kept the aliens from controlling him as they controlled Molly.

The aliens had driven Molly outside just now, luring Landon out into the open. To suck him into their secret gate. He shivered and hastened his step, sliding on a rock that sent off a mini avalanche of scattering rocks.

He kicked a rock aside and dropped down onto his hands and knees beside Aquilino, who crouched in a shallow gully that seeped under the hut.

"Zsssst," the guide said, holding his finger to his lips. His gaze drifted to a crevice that split open the rocky hillside several meters away. Moonlight illuminated the edge of the crevice, meeting deep shadows of a small cave.

Something moved inside the shadows.

Molly.

Just as Landon opened his mouth to cry out her name, the guide's rough hand, smelling of the earth, clamped over his nostrils and mouth. The cry gurgled and died in his throat.

"Let her hear El Pastor," Aquilino whispered, removing his hand from Landon's face.

Landon shook off Aquilino and scrambled away, clawing through piles of leaves and vines and seeds and roots as he moved through the springy tangle up the gully toward the crevice.

"No!" Aquilino called out from behind him.

Movement in the shadows of the crevice revealed Molly as she crawled out from the rocky den. She cradled something small in one arm and gently set it down in a silvery ray of moonlight. A bird, lying on its side. A seagull. Except, he didn't think it was alive.

As the moonlight touched it, lying there, its feathers quivered. One eyeball unrolled, opening.

Landon sucked in his breath and slid backwards, closer to Aquilino. "What's wrong with it?"

"Belong to El Pastor. Why he no need Doctor Chan's talk machine."

Just then, a sharp zinging sound split the air. Aquilino cried out. Landon whipped around in time to see the guide fall backwards.

Landon knew the sound of a gun. He hugged the ground, diving behind boulders. The shot had come from the rocks above the goat pen. "Molly, get back!"

The guide clutched his chest, slumping to the ground. The bird, bathed in moonlight, lifted into the air, flapped its wings, and soared away, in the direction of where the gunshot had fired.

"Aquilino!" Landon nudged closer, flinging Molly's coat onto him to stanch the flow of blood.

"You...stop them," Aquilino said, shuddering. "Is...too late...for me."

"I can't leave you," Landon said. He peered around the boulder. Silhouetted against the moonlight, the shape of a man in a jumpsuit held a weapon and rose up from the rocks above the goat pen. The bird soared close, dive-bombing his head. The man fired a wild shot into the air, and the seagull dove again, screaming and chittering.

Molly crawled the rest of the way out of the cave that had hidden her and the bird. She rolled down into the gully toward Landon's protective arms but not close enough for him to reach her.

"Get down, honey!" he yelled at her as he turned to look back at Aquilino. He had to help the guide fast before he bled to death, but he also had to protect Molly. He wished she would've just stayed hidden in that cave until he could come for her. But no.

The bird screamed again, flapping its wings with a drumming sound of blades pounding the air. The gunman cursed, kicking off tumbling rocks, and the goats bleated and frisked. The weapon fired again, clattering to the rocky ground.

Molly sprang to her feet and darted away with a speed greater than any two-year-old should have.

"Molly!" Landon called. "Come back!"

"Go..." Aquilino whispered. "Follow her..." As if willing his life's essence to slip away, he slumped into silence.

CHAPTER TWENTY-FOUR

SUMMER'S SKIN CRAWLED with shivers as El Pastor's eyes rolled back in his head, exposing the whites of his eyes.

"Have no fear," he — or she — said-sang in a woman's voice. A Tititri voice. An *alien*.

Summer curled her toes inside her boots and ground them into the floor of sponge, inside this cavern, deep under the cover of glacier. Her knees quivered, but she locked them in place, refusing to collapse into the puddle of fear that the alien seemed to expect from her. Against a backdrop of shadows pumping up and down and gears rumbling and clicking, she could see the upright figure of the vine-draped shaman well enough.

And hear him. Or her.

His sing-song voice was the same woman's voice who had spoken to Summer before. She'd thought it was the moon voice. A healer. She should've known that any voice sliding down a moonbeam into her ear implants would've been that of...an *alien*.

All along... The alien had been touching her thoughts.

She shivered. Her heartbeat faltered. Shudders ran through her torso, filthy from the touch of...an *alien*. She swayed, shaking her knees loose from their lock. There was no such thing as a healer for Summer. But there *were* aliens. She'd tried to help in the effort to keep aliens from coming as she'd feared all along that they would. But she'd failed. She'd fallen into the alien's lair. Because Diamond shoved her, betraying her.

Diamond... Her supposed friend who was no friend. He was as contaminated as the rest of them.

El Pastor's rocking motion stopped. His head tipped downward, aiming the whites of his eyes in her direction. The alien's silky voice spoke from within El Pastor. "They mean you no harm."

She rooted into her spot, as well as she could stabilize herself on the non-firm surface. *They?* The alien wasn't speaking to her, then. But who was? Whoever, the female-sounding voice within El Pastor was surely talking about aliens.

"They have no right to mean anything for me," she said, forcing strength into her whispery voice, making herself sound more belligerent than the weakling she felt she was. She wouldn't let any aliens think they'd intimidated her, no matter what El Pastor really was. "They've already taken my family, my life. What more can they possibly take away from me? What else do they want?"

Summer's voice did not sound like hers, not as she remembered. She did not think she spoke in her language, and yet, she knew that she somehow conveyed her meaning.

"They are not here to take away from you but to give to all." The woman's voice singing through El Pastor sounded hypnotic, like the babbling tinkling mellifluous sounds of the tumbling waters of a mountain stream, and it lulled the trembles riddling Summer's mind. "The Tititri only wish to co-habitate. In peace. They shelter your people as you shelter theirs."

"Oh," Summer said. That didn't sound so bad. She could

understand that. It was the dream of idealists, wasn't it? But she didn't believe it was that simple. For one thing, there was no room on Earth for idealists anymore. "You speak of them as if you are not one of them." She felt like a petulant child, shrinking within herself, yet thrusting her chin up and out, daring the thing that controlled El Pastor to contradict her. Wishing it would.

The whites of El Pastor's eyes flickered, reflecting the subdued light that seeped around the edges of shadows. "I was built by their ancestors to monitor their great migration. And now it comes to pass. They call my sentience the PRI, a Tititri term for protector. You are also a PRI."

"I am no such thing!" Summer felt herself clench, a moment frozen in time. She was not a built thing. Machines were built. But what if the Savers' ear implants had made her machine-like? Her heart skipped a beat, reminding her that she was alive, not an alien machine.

It went on. "Survival is the higher order. Survival is the goal of all life, yours as well as theirs. That is why they have brought you here to receive them. You are the chosen protector, the guardian."

Receive *aliens?* When all her life she had worked hard with the Savers to keep aliens from coming! Her reward for that was prison in Patagonia. And in the end, after the sacrifice of her life, of her husband and child, she'd failed. Aliens were coming, anyway. Now they had the nerve to want protection from *her.*

"Protect them how?" Summer didn't feel like much of a protector. She'd failed at that job, over and over.

"It was all for the purpose of bringing you here to Patagonia, where you are needed." He — no, he was a machine, an *it* —

spoke as if it had read her mind.

Here. She glanced around herself in the dark, at the shadowy, whispering shapes. A spongy floor; cycling, shifting gears. Her life's destination. She was a prisoner to this dark place, this alien-built machine under a glacier.

All along, she'd thought she was working to save Earth from the forthcoming invasion of aliens. That's what the Savers had promised her when they recruited her to their cause.

But it was a lie.

The aliens had been here all along. Here, under the glacier. All her life, they had been luring her here to their lair in Patagonia. They'd been controlling the choices in life she'd made that had brought her here.

Trembles racked her body, rejecting the alien contamination. She felt soiled inside out.

Then another thought tumbled through her mind. The Savers who'd recruited her... Were *they*, in fact, the aliens?

Laughter tickled Summer's mind along with her realization. Laughter tinkled along like wind chimes as the machine speaking through El Pastor sing-sang in the moon voice. Summer feared she'd fallen into the deep dark of her own subconscious.

No... The laughter wasn't coming from within her. It seemed to be coming from the spinning circles of the darkness that *surrounded* her. It was alien laughter, and it lodged here, in this buried, alien-made machine.

Summer looked up at the silent shapes of tumbling gears, cycling round and round. Watching them made her own head spin.

"Follow me," the machine voice said, and El Pastor turned toward the circle of gnashing shapes that surrounded them.

Or perhaps the pumping shapes closed in on her. Fear at being left alone in this place seized her, propelling her after the shaman's movement. Her feet floated through air. The spongy surface of the floor seemed to guide her not only through the cinnamon air but also past the shifting, churning shapes. They parted and reformed as she float-stepped, spinning and tumbling, round and round.

It was not she who moved but the circles of tooth-like prongs that spun around her. Dizzy, she felt as if she were inside a giant system of gears. Luminescence floated like fireflies snagged by each prong. Luminescence had produced the muted light in this otherwise dark cavern well beneath the glacier.

"What *is* this place?" she asked, her stomach roiling.

"One of many storage areas for the Tititri blueprints."

"Blueprints of what?"

"Of their bodies."

She tested her feet, her uncertain balance, and took a step closer to El Pastor, the only quasi-familiar object in this alien den. "Why *me*?" Because of Landon, she would bet her life on it. He, too, had spoken of blueprints, having something to do with the incomprehensible machines he'd built.

"They need us PRIs."

"But I am not a machine," she said, feeling silly talking to a machine, while standing before the vine-clad shape of the shaman, inside a giant mechanism that stored aliens. "If you're a machine, then where are you? Why do you hide within El Pastor? Let him go!"

"My physical receptacle lodges on your moon as one half of two sister entities. The ancestors of the Titinha built us long ago, in the days before ice covered your world. One of us was sent to your moon to observe conditions on your world, while the other of us descended into the tunnels inside your world. We have waited many cycles of lying dormant, for the time to be right, the time when the Titinha would activate us."

"Ti...tinha? Not Tititri?"

"The Titinha is the inherited leader who decides the fate of the Tititri and speaks through PRI."

"So, you're telling me this on Titinha's behalf?" Summer and her Savers had only been trying to protect Earth from the alien invasion. And yet, the aliens had been here all along. All along *she* had been doing what the aliens bid her to do. The Savers were not really Earth's savers at all. The Savers were more like facilitators. "The invasion has already begun?"

"Not an invasion," said the female-sounding voice of the alien machine through El Pastor's lips. "The Tititri have come far, too far for their delicate life form to travel. They have been searching for a new home for the people, who merely seek refuge."

It sounded like an invasion to her. And Summer had brought them here. Already, they'd taken El Pastor.

"The Tititri will not trouble you. They seek refuge from the invading Xyvors, from whom the Tititri flee. The Xyvors will not bother with a single star. Your sun, alone, generates none of the power of orbital dynamics that the Xyvors seek from multiple star systems. They use such power to fuel their needs, at the cost of any lifeforms in their way. Your simple sun will not lure them here. Your people and Tititri can coexist in safety."

But that wasn't true. There was no safety for anyone, not anymore, not ever. Summer's pulse hammered in her head. Why did everyone lie to her? El Pastor lied, too. Her entire *life* was a lie.

"Blueprints are in storage now," the alien machine said through El Pastor's lips, "but once the leader Titinha emerges, new platforms will be constructed for Tititri to inhabit. The PRI mission means to control a select group of humans — yourself, being one. Your people are being instructed to carry out the task of growing new bodies for the Tititri on which to implant their blueprints. Then your work as a PRI will cease, and you will be released along with your daughter. The Tititri will need not bother your people any longer, and the Xyvors will turn away from this sector of the galaxy, seeking elsewhere for the power they require."

Summer was no longer sure of what she heard or what she imagined. She did not remember creating the Xyvors in her imagination.

Xyvors... A mispronunciation of Savers? They were the same.

A small sigh escaped her, steadying her on her uncertain feet, facing El Pastor within the spinning circle shapes. She'd known it was all a lie. Because her daughter... Molilia was not here. Her daughter had already died, elsewhere. Somewhere away, far away.

"You have served us well," said the voice of the aliens, "but your real purpose is only now beginning."

She shuddered. They wanted even more of her. She was nothing but an alien puppet, when all along... She could not! No, no, no! She would not take anymore. She would not let any aliens determine her fate for her. She would not abide them.

She would release herself from them. There was a way...

El Pastor's vines would help her.

177

CHAPTER TWENTY-FIVE

SHIT, GREER THOUGHT. It was her fault.

She was the one who'd practically sent Molly outside to play with the seagulls. Aliens. That's where the aliens were hiding — inside the birds.

A tick twitched Greer's eyebrow. Her glance slipped off Brant the warden guy's hunky shoulders and darted over to the blinking, blipping machines going swoosh. She shivered. "You must have some sort of way to phone them in all that mess of stuff. You've got to bring them back inside."

He laughed. He actually laughed. But it wasn't funny.

"You think this operation is for mere security purposes?" he said, waving his arm to indicate the cold room with its steel wall of body drawers and the array of pulsing machines.

Pulse! That's what the sound was. Like the heartbeat of bodies that weren't quite dead yet.

She tried to make her voice sound light, but it came out a bit too high-pitched squeaky. "You have to keep track of everyone's movements in a high-security place like this, right? I just thought —"

"You thought wrong. Trust me, you will not find a way to crack our security and help your brother's wife escape. She cannot escape us. Now I suggest you find your earring before I call the guards."

"Escape!" Greer's voice shot even higher. "I'm not trying to help her escape. She can stay in prison and rot, for all I care."

"A likely scenario."

"I only care about Molly. And Landon. They shouldn't be outside." Where the bird-aliens could get them.

"They are well guarded."

"By an escort. That's what you called him before," Greer said.

"Indeed. You would not want to meet an actual guard."

"But what about the escorts?"

"What about them?" His voice lowered to the gruff range.

"Yeah, like the one outside with Landon and Molly." She hoped to distract Brant from the subject of aliens. *He'd* been the first one to bring up the matter of escorts. Not her. "How many of that sort do you have working here?"

"As many as it takes."

"To control your prisoners, you mean?"

"Everything is about control here. Control is the point."

"Then, you've got to call them back. Now. Before…"

Oops. She wasn't allowed to talk about the aliens. Landon would kill her if she gave away his precious secret, the reason behind ISA's top secret mission.

"Before what?"

"Before they catch cold!" She knew it sounded unconvincing, but she couldn't talk sense while she was thinking, and right now her mind was roiling like a North Sea storm.

Molly had toddled down the hall as if she'd known exactly where she was going — here, into this very room. But it wasn't Molly directing herself. It was the alien inside Molly. The alien who'd spoken to all of them the night before when they'd chased that crazy jungle woman — Ziza — who'd stolen Molly. And now the alien was inside a bird that Molly was chasing after.

"I fear it's too late for that," Brant said with another evil-sounding chuckle. "The wind has come up."

Greer shivered, feeling as if the Patagonian wind had penetrated the cement building and whipped straight into her heart. Or maybe that was the alien trying to control *her*, too?

The alien meant for Molly to come into this very room, and then what? Molly somehow turned off these blipping machines. But it wasn't Molly. It was the alien inside Molly. Or inside the bird. Had it done some sort of mind link? Was that how?

"The wind will chase them back inside," he said, but she wasn't paying much attention to his words. Because she was trying to figure out...

How...?

How didn't matter. It was why. Why didn't Molly's alien want these machines to blip and squiggle? Why turn them off? Why now? Greer peered at the screens flashing patterns and smatters of color. Spinning cubes, and —

"Hey!" she cried out, pointing at the monitor showing some sort of picture of an interior. "That's Summer! But...but... What's she doing there? Where is she?"

Brant swept past her, nearly knocking her over with his haste. With his body, he blocked the image of Summer on the screen.

Maybe she'd been mistaken, and it wasn't really Summer.

But she didn't think so. The image had been fuzzy, but she would recognize Summer's willowy silhouette anywhere, even wearing an orange prison jumpsuit. Her bushy, untamed hair gave her away. Landon's ex-wife had always moved as if on tiptoes, slightly hunched over. How many people — especially, prisoners down here — carried themselves with that same gait?

But what was she doing on the monitor's screen? Director General Manrique had made a point of saying that Summer was away on some sort of exercise duty. If that was the case, then her duty was connected to this room.

Greer had always suspected something fishy about this room.

She bet the aliens did, too.

Or else, this room was a gateway of sorts, to the aliens. That's why Molly had been drawn here! The aliens were calling her to them.

And she bet the gate was hiding behind those handles of what looked like body drawers and smelled yeasty, like Aunt Jewel's freshly baked cardamom bread.

Well.

They were doors. For seagulls. Not drawers.

Brant fiddled with his machines, acting as if he'd completely forgotten the presence of Greer. The image of Summer had rattled him. As if maybe she wasn't supposed to show up on his screens.

Whatever.

Now was Greer's chance. She tiptoed swiftly to the wall of doors and reached for the nearest handle.

CHAPTER TWENTY-SIX

LANDON KEPT THE SEAGULL in sight overhead as he raced across tundra. In the moonlight, everything changed. The flight of the bird looked like a beacon's light, sweeping along through the dark, guiding him.

Guiding Molly, too.

In the moonlight, the alien took over Molly's toddler body, and the seagull led her across glacier-scarred terrain unfit for a child scarcely past learning to walk. If Landon was to prevent the alien from controlling Molly, he would have to get her out of the moonlight. Something, he suspected, was broadcasting from the moon to activate all this.

The bird.

The alien that drove Molly.

Tripping over rocks, righting his balance, he lurched onward. The cold of the frozen turf seared through his boots. His hammering feet sent stabs of numbing pain upward through his body. Pain clenched his lungs.

Gasping...

If the beacon guided both Molly and Landon, then it would aid Aquilino's killer too, lurking somewhere behind a rock or the crest of a hill. Stalking them. What would he do to Molly if he caught her first? He'd already killed the harmless guide. The eagle, the goat whisperer, Aquilino had done nothing but help Landon.

He'd even died intercepting a bullet meant for Landon.

Despite the throb in Landon's shoulder, reminding him how narrowly he'd escaped the same fate only the night before, he ran harder. He had to stop such evil before the killer stopped him from saving Molly.

Landon had *thought* he'd already saved his daughter. It felt as if last night in the jungle was happening all over again. Last night seemed like another lifetime ago.

And now the killer was somewhere out there, chasing both of them.

The killer's attention surely fixed mostly on Molly. Perhaps it was the killer's job to push Molly along, to see that she reached her destination, wherever it was that the bird guided her.

At times, Landon caught a glimpse of both shadowy figures in the far distance. Molly seemed to know exactly where she was going. Landon thought his mind must be playing tricks on him, leaving him lightheaded. Probably a result of oxygen deprivation at this altitude.

It was ironic... Wrestling with a battering wind.

Gusts roared down from the soaring mountain peaks, pushing him away from where Molly seemed headed. But then he realized such deceptions were probably the green-eyed alien's doing, the thing called the Titinha who controlled Molly's little body.

He had no idea why his daughter had been caught up in all this. Nor what she had to do with any aliens. What could they possibly want from her?

The wind pushed him to a standstill. Yes, he did know. It

was past time for him to acknowledge the truths he'd long tried to deny. A chilling wave of understanding washed over him, penetrating to his bones.

Summer. He realized it was Summer. Molly's mother had been the link between Molly and the aliens.

Molly, in utero, had been an innocent bystander to the alien takeover of Summer. Perhaps the aliens had engineered Molly from that initial union of his sperm and Summer's egg.

And if the aliens could do all that, then Landon wondered if they were driving *him* as well. The seagull had lured them up the mountain. He'd practically brought Molly into the waiting arms of Aquilino's killer, who was probably also controlled by the aliens. Because the killer was propelling Molly to the aliens, guided by their bird. Contact between them would somehow complete the transformation of Molly into alien.

Back to his original question: *why?* Why were the Tititri going to such lengths? What did they want of Molly?

Landon tucked his chin down and rammed his head into the wind, pushing on. He didn't have time to wonder why. He had to get Molly back. Now.

But no matter how fast he managed to run, pushing against the wind, the distance spread farther between him and his daughter. As Landon's body lurched over uneven terrain, his mind churned, trying to understand all that transpired around him. None of it made sense.

Landon had thought all along that the "bad ones" Aquilino had referenced must've been the Tititri. Clearly, the killer was *the* bad one, and surely the guide had meant him. Either Landon had interpreted the wrong message from the guide or else the killer was a Tititri. If the latter, then its shape looked humanoid.

If all the Tititri were humanoid, then Landon would have a devil of a time recognizing whom he had to fight.

He assumed he had to fight them. H.F. had warned about their imminent invasion. That's why Landon was here now, struggling across these Patagonian mountains in air that was scarcely breathable. H.F. claimed the aliens had an outpost here.

Perhaps that was where the bird was directing Molly now.

And the killer, who might be Tititri.

A shudder rippled through him, maybe from pain, maybe from adrenaline. Summer had known all along about the threat of aliens. He'd thought she was crazy.

He'd been wrong.

The shudder made him stumble, and he wondered if he was far enough out of range of the killer's weapon. The killer would aim for him again, if he knew Landon was out here too.

He would know.

Because a father would do everything in his power to get his daughter back. If an alien controlled the killer, or even if he was a humanoid alien, he or it would possess abilities that Landon couldn't even imagine.

But somehow, he would defeat them. He had to. To get Molly back.

Landon felt sure he was heading into a trap, but he had no choice. He had to rescue his daughter. Again.

The seagull soared above a debris field, littered with boulders and chunks of ice, an obstacle that spread across the route Landon needed to take, if he was to follow the bird and Molly. He picked his way maddeningly slowly, wondering how a child could progress more easily, disappearing from sight on the far side.

Landon lunged on.

A rectangular shape loomed ahead. Its edges appeared too perfectly refined to be anything natural. It wasn't a tower of rocks, nor a cylindrically shaped mountain peak. It appeared man-made. The seagull swooped toward the cylinder and perched atop it, as if waiting for Landon to catch up.

Towers.

They were towers. Tips of towers protruding from the glacier.

A chill gripped his lungs. Ice from the air seeped along his spine. He thought his heart had frozen in mid-beat. A picture of those other towers flashed through his mind, the alien ruins of towers he'd found on Titan during his mission there. These looked the same, resembling the shape of a cityscape's outline. Except this shape was not that of a full city but only a few skyscrapers. Three or four.

These couldn't be the same. This was Earth, not Titan, no matter that he felt frozen here. His eco suit back on Titan had kept him from feeling the cold temperatures there. He'd actually stayed warmer on Titan than here in the Patagonian mountains. Now, his jacket hung askew, ripped and tugged by the wind. He'd been in too much rush leaving the goatherder's hut to put the jacket on properly and fasten it against the wind and cold.

And what of Molly, with no jacket at all?

As he ran the last of the distance, he tugged at the fasteners and pulled up the head gear and retracted the hand warmers. The shadowy figure of Molly rose up from the horizon, in the distance against the moonlight, and approached the tower where the seagull perched. Then her shape disappeared, as if she'd walked straight into the tower. The tower had somehow absorbed her.

Landon lunged forward, toward the piece of the cityscape that contained the apparent entrance. The seagull wailed and flapped its wings, as if it tried to warn Landon away. Or else warn someone — some*thing* — of his approach.

He pressed on, trying to catch up to the spot where Molly had been swallowed into the tower. He tried to keep his focus pinned onto that spot, despite his up and down motion as he half ran half stumbled.

Edging closer, he slowed to step carefully around sinkholes, where the ice had cracked apart. He remembered having fallen through a similar hole on Titan. He wondered how long the aliens had been here on Earth. Maybe they had come here after discovering Titan's inhospitable offerings.

Where these towers rose high into the night sky, he found the entrance to an ice cave, which tunneled in the direction of the tower's base. The terrain was smoother here, tramped down, perhaps, by others passing this way before. He wanted to race inside, but if the killer lurked there, waiting for him, then Landon would become an easy, point-blank target.

Instead, he dove behind a chunk of ice at the entrance to the cave and shouted. "Molly!"

There was no need for quiet. The killer must already know Landon was on Molly's trail. Instead, Landon wanted to let his daughter know that he was coming. She was all that mattered, all he cared about.

The reminder, though, made him take more caution. He couldn't get himself killed before rescuing Molly.

He strained to listen for a sound, any sound out of place beneath the howl of the wind. A whimper from Molly, or a gurgle, or one of her babble streams. The sound of the killer's heavy breathing.

Nothing.

He would do no good crouching behind a chunk of ice. He crept forward, scooped up a fistful of ice and pebbles and tossed them into the dark mouth of the ice cave. Nothing responded, no shots, no cries of alarm.

He extended his gloved fist around the edge of the ice cave's wall.

Silence.

Encouraged, he crunched forward another step into the dark. He smelled the air.

Nothing but the smell of ice and earth.

He waited, listening for the click of a weapon, waiting for the feel of rising hairs on the back of his neck, rising from the nearness of a predator, but nothing came to him, and so he continued, groping with one arm outstretched before him. The other arm slid along the icy side of the cave's wall. Slowly, his eyesight adjusted to the dark, and he could make out the jagged sides of the ice cave, angling toward a circle of blankness at the back of the cave.

It was a hole, tunneling deep under the glacier. Or maybe under the wall of the tower.

He pressed closer, but the circle of dark did not resolve into anything he could recognize.

And then his feet dropped beneath him, as if a force below had caught them and yanked, pulling him down, and he was falling, feet first... Weightlessness encased him, shedding his pounds as in freefall. A breeze whistled off his jacket and ruffled his eyelashes, pressing his eyelids half closed. He would die when he touched bottom, but he couldn't die, not yet. He had to rescue Molly.

As suddenly as his falling had started, the motion stopped. Now he lay panting, swaddled in a foam-like softness. His arms flailed about him, and the foam released its embrace. He tried to push himself upright, onto his feet, but dizziness toppled him to his knees. He panted some more, shook his head, trying to shake off the dizziness, and slowly rose.

A pleasant fragrance warmed him, reminding him of warm memories. It was...the bakery his father had taken him and Greer to, back in Vancouver, in another world lost in time.

"Dad?"

The word slipped out before his reason could override it. Of course his father wasn't here. His father had died in the bombing of the sports dome long ago.

It was his daughter he expected to find here. Not his father.

Gradually, he perceived a soft glow, faintly illuminating the space around him. He couldn't pinpoint the light's source, but it was just enough to allow him to see the cavernous space surrounding him, disappearing into shadows.

"You must stop him," said a voice with an echo.

Someone...here with him!

Yes, of course. This place must be the alien outpost. The aliens had brought Molly here. One of them spoke to him now.

He could not determine gender from the even tone of the voice, nor could he see the shape of the speaker. It almost sounded like an early mechanical. With the echo, he did not know where the voice originated. He whirled around, feeling as if he swam through his dizziness. "Molly!" he called out.

His own voice did not echo.

He listened for the sound of her movement, her tiny feet, her soft sighs. Instead, he heard a faint rumble, a low thrum of machines working somewhere in the distance. He hoped it was a ventilation system or some other form of life support. He had no idea how far under he'd fallen or how much time had elapsed during his fall to estimate a calculation of distance. He felt dizzy from disorientation.

"Who are you, that you know what I have to do?" he shouted at the genderless voice in the shadows. "Where are you? Come out, so that I can see you." He listened again to the faint thrum. It seemed to grow louder, a buzz in his head.

He glanced around, scanning the dark, searching for an exit. He'd entered this place, so there must be a way out. His martial arts training had taught him that in any situation he should always know where the exit was, relative to his position. He hoped there was another way out other than the hole in the ceiling he'd apparently fallen through. He should be dead.

Maybe he *was* dead.

"Where's Molly?" His voice rose with frustration, but still it did not echo.

"The host is safe for now, but only if you stop him. If not, everyone dies."

She was a *host*. For some *thing* that had invaded her. An alien. A Tititri. A wave of nausea spread through him. "She's just a baby," he shouted back at the thing that seemed to know about Molly's possession. It was another Tititri. He shook off his dizziness and sprang to his wobbling feet. "I'm taking her back."

"You may not have her."

A growl slid from his throat. Nothing, no one, would stop him, not as long as breath remained in his body. He narrowed his eyes, willing his vision to penetrate the gloom, making out shadowy shapes that spun around him. He leaned in the direction he wished to move, but his feet felt out of sync with the movements of the rest of his body and would not follow. He shifted his weight onto the balls of his feet, loosening himself from the sensation of sludge holding him down. Now he could bounce forward a little easier.

"No," said the voice without gender. "No...no..." It echoed.

Landon thrashed, first one way and then the other, trying to chase the echoes, but his movement felt restrained, in the same manner as if he were plunging through a pool of water. His erratic motion finally brought into view the shadowy outline of a tall, upright person. It was either an observer or the person who'd spoken, the person who refused to turn Molly over to him.

Landon cried out and funneled all of his strength into a lunge toward the shadow. His momentum kept him going, and he charged into something silky, feeling much like the animal fur of the goat hides back in the goatherder's hut.

The memory of Aquilino's death there pumped adrenaline through him, and he tackled his foe, the being who stood between father and daughter. He threw his object down to the ensnaring ground and knelt over him, pinning down his prisoner's torso. It felt like a goat's. But at this close range, the face of a man resolved in the shadowy gloom.

No...

Not a man, but a creature. White eyeballs glittered up at

him. For an instant he thought it was half goat half man. Its breath unleashed a rotting smell, the smell of corpses in the aftermath of the sports dome bombing, and they washed over Landon's face.

He recoiled, and his flinch released his prisoner. The creature crawled away, toward the shadows, but Landon scrambled faster, and he caught the edge of the goat hides that wrapped the being. His target. But not Aquilino's killer who had followed — or directed — Molly here. At least, he didn't think so.

"Where is she?" Landon shouted, yanking fistfuls of fur.

The goat hides slipped off the creature's shoulders, pulling looping ropes along with them, revealing...not an alien being at all but an old, wizened man. Huddled on the ground, he shivered in an underwear liner, similar to what Landon wore under a spacesuit. From the waist-length of his matted, gray hair it appeared that he'd never had a haircut — and from the smell of him, possibly not a bath — in his lifetime, which Landon judged to be close to a century.

The old man's eyeballs quivered, and then the whites rolled, dropping dark pupils back into place. He sighed and shook himself and squinted at Landon. "So you have come," the old man said in a husky, male voice, a *different* sound from the neutral, echoing voice of a few minutes ago. "As they predicted. They told me you might come."

"Who told you? The Tititri?" Considering the change in the goat man's voice, Landon figured the aliens must use him, too. "Are they with her now? Where are they holding her?"

"I do not know." He sighed again. "They are gone. Perhaps they have already taken her through the gate."

A chill slid through Landon, and he shivered. Aquilino had spoken of a secret gate to another place, a gate that El Pastor guarded. "Are you the one they call El Pastor?"

The old man nodded, wincing, as if his admission pained him.

Landon's heart squeezed. He released his grip on El Pastor and helped him to his feet. The goatherder had failed in his guardian mission as badly as Landon had failed the people who mattered most in his life. "Tell me about this gate."

"It is the door to the place where the girl can grow, safe."

"Safe?" That was all Landon could hope for his daughter, to be safe. "Why would they take her away through your gate if it's me they want? That's what Aquilino said. Someone's after *me*." He tilted his chin up to shout into the shadows above. "Here I am! Why don't you take me and leave her alone? She's just a child."

El Pastor clutched at him. "You must go away from here. They will kill you to keep their secret safe while the girl grows."

"Their secret *is* safe, since I don't know what it is. They're aliens, that's all I know, but I can't see them." He couldn't fight anyone if he did not know whom to fight. But hope resurfaced, as the old man's words — *go away from here* — implied there actually was an exit from this place. He would find it and take Molly through it.

"You do not understand."

"Darned right, I don't. I don't even know what this place is. How could I know what's going on here? Is it the work of someone at the prison?" Manrique. Chan. Hermanson.

El Pastor's head dipped in what might have been a nod. "Me and my goats, we found the things poking out of ice when it start to melt. I never saw anything like it before, not ever, so I told Doctor Chan down there at prison. She is smart woman, maybe she knows what it is. She called her boss, brought team of Executors all the way from that place across sea. They come here, but I did not show them the gate."

"Why not?"

"The grasses told me not to." El Pastor reached for the looping ropes that had unrolled from his shoulders along with the goat hides.

Landon snatched up the ropes of braided grasses, quicker than El Pastor could reach them, and he wrapped them as a trophy around his own arm. "What else did your grass tell you?"

Talking grass. This place, whatever it was — the Tititri outpost H.F. had warned him about — must be getting to him. Or else the flares of memories about his ex-wife were doing the job. To entertain such notions made him sound as crazy as Summer.

Then, understanding washed over him. If the people from the prison were guarding this alien place for whatever reason, then Summer's exercise duty must be connected to it.

He lifted his voice, calling into the dark. "Summer!" He guessed she was here somewhere.

He paused, waiting for her to respond. Nothing. He listened for any small sounds — a soft breath, a rustle of clothing, a snap of joints — anything that might give away her presence. Nothing.

"They've got Molly," he called to Summer in the thrumming darkness, in case she was listening. He suspected she was. "Come out. We can work together on this. We both want what's best for her, don't we?"

Silence. Not even an echo responded.

But he sensed her presence.

He shuddered again. The alien within Molly wouldn't care about what was best for his daughter. It called itself the Titinha and said it would release Molly when "they" were done. But would it? And even if it did, its impact on Molly for the rest of her life was unfathomable. Landon wasn't sure he could trust an alien to keep its word. The alien would greet the rest of the Tititri who were preparing to invade Earth.

Not only did Landon have to save his child, but he also had to save Earth.

It was more than he could do. More than any ordinary human could do. He wanted to crumble into a thousand pieces, hammered down by the weight of such responsibility. He wanted to scream his pain, eating away at him cell by cell. He wanted to sink into the shadows and let the darkness suffocate him with its icy fingers. He wanted to die.

No.

No he did *not*. He wanted to live. He wanted humanity to live. He wanted Molly.

He spun in circles, searching for the first step toward what he must do. The gate. The old man thought "they" had taken Molly through it because he'd failed to guard it.

"Where is this gate of yours?" Landon said. Renewed confidence streamed through him, fueling him with the strength he would need.

The old man's tongue ticked at him, scolding him. "If you open door to gate, we all die."

"If you won't tell me, then I'll find it on my own."

Landon didn't even know what he was looking for. He had a

perception of what doors and gates looked like, but he suspected that whatever gate El Pastor was talking about looked nothing like anything from Landon's experience. He turned away from the ragged breathing sounds of the old man and fell into the dark.

He moved one way, and the mechanical thrums grew fainter. He turned the opposite direction, following the increasing intensity of the vibrating hum, careful not to stumble across El Pastor, but his new course was apparently yet a different direction. The old man did not lie in this path. His fetid breath evaporated, and its rasping gasps faded away. A new smell replaced the foul air, reminding Landon once again of the bakery. A sensation of warmth chased away the chills shivering through him.

"No!" El Pastor's cries sounded far away.

The hairs on the back of Landon's neck rose, as if electricity flowed through him. Careful not to touch anything, he paused and scanned the dark. Something flickered at him ahead to the right.

He shuffled forward a few more steps, slightly right, and then stopped again. The dark wasn't so dark as it had been originally. Now he could see a series of shapes outlining rectangles and triangles and circles.

A pinprick of light leaked out from the junction of shapes, showing him the way. Then he sucked in his breath, recognizing the pattern of shapes and the way they interlocked together. Even the shade of greenish blue of the leaking light was the same ethereal shade as...

Impossible.

It was the same machine...

One of Van Pelt's...

A prototype, he'd thought, and he'd seen it himself, only last year, in Van Pelt's laboratory... Landon had gone there, calling on his colleague to discuss the problem of the tachyonic emission, streaming towards Earth from the direction of the Centauri system. But that discussion never happened, because he'd found Van Pelt's dead body.

What was his blueprint receiver doing *here*?

CHAPTER TWENTY-SEVEN

"WE ARE ALMOST THERE," the voice of Ziza-Hybrid told the footsteps pattering along behind them, trying to keep up with her blazing pace through the jungle. "To the jumping place."

Her voice and understanding were growing with each leaping footfall, thanks to the assistance of the original formerly known as Ziza Fonseca, whose essence lodged deep within the body, inside the parasite's nest.

She knew now, for instance, that the streak of red who pierced the green was known as parrot. The parrot screamed at her, all the while leading the way of her path to the jumping place.

Ziza-Hybrid knew about this green world, her new world. Soon, it would not be possible for an outside observer to notice anything alien about the human body once known as Ziza Fonseca.

Perhaps the mother who had birthed her would notice, but Mãe was dead. Killed by PRI, the Titinha's protector partner, killed as a threat to the Titinha's plan. It was a plan that not all Tititri desired.

Ziza-Hybrid ran faster, commanding her new muscles to lift the mud-blocked feet and sail them through the wet air. Faster, harder, onward. She had to get there, to the jumping place. She could not allow PRI to kill again. The Tititri needed these human bodies if they were to survive.

The Xyvors, on the other hand, did not wish for any life to survive that was not Xyvor.

Ziza-Hybrid felt safe, finally, in her new world. It was dark in a green way, as compared to the Tititri's world of Ti, which was dark in an angry, red way. Dark, angry, and red, on account of the Xyvors, the hated, dreaded warriors who advanced through the galaxy, growing stronger and more hateful with each new solar conquest.

From deep within her former body, Ziza, who was now parasite, understood. It was the same for her mother's people, the Mundomba, when the re-educators swept through Mãe's jungle, stealing Mundomba power in the form of plants and animals. Only this pocket of jungle remained, protecting its secrets.

Ziza-Hybrid knew the way. That knowledge was imbedded within her blueprint, transferred from the blueprint-maker that the human had brought to Ti through a rip in time and the dissidents had stolen.

It could not fail.

They were almost there, to the heart of the secret. And then the red streak sailed to a stop. Its banner of red vanished as the parrot alighted atop a stone rising up from the green. It turned to scream at her. But Ziza-Hybrid would not let it stop her from jumping, not now that she had finally reached this circle of standing stones.

CHAPTER TWENTY-EIGHT

A CHARGE BOLTED THROUGH Greer as she grasped the handle of the body drawer in Doctor Chan's off-limits laboratory. The crackle of electricity lifted the hair from the nape of her neck and threw her backwards. "Oh!" she cried, tumbling onto her butt and sliding across the slick floor.

Brant the hunky warden bodyguard turned at the zapping, crashing commotion she'd made and practically snarled. "I told you not to touch that. Can't you ever listen?"

She panted, trying to catch her breath. "Holy shit! What was that?"

"Nothing that you need to know about."

"It tried to kill me! You might've told me, y'know."

"I did."

"No you didn't. You didn't say it would try to *kill* me. That's different from just being your stupid secret." Her entire body trembled. She couldn't stop shaking. She heaved, panting, and all Brant did was stand there frowning down at her. He might've at least asked if she was all right.

No. She wasn't, thank you very much.

She rolled over onto her hands and knees, giving him a glimpse of her ass. But still, he didn't offer a helping hand.

Well. Maybe he wasn't so hunky after all.

She pushed herself up to stand on wobbling knees and turned to face the inconsiderate jerk. Completely ignoring her, he cursed at the squiggling lines on his monitors and crouched like a panther, ready to pounce on another machine. His face looked genuinely worried the way it wrinkled up. His icy blue eyes stared at those stupid machines as if he could actually see inside to the inner workings.

Apparently, he didn't like what he saw.

Had Greer done something to mess things up? Just by getting herself nearly electrocuted?

Served him right, didn't it? He might've told her. If this stuff was so dangerous, where was the skull and crossbones sign, huh?

Although, now that she thought about it, maybe it was time for her to leave.

"Never mind about my missing earring," she said, sidling over to the exit. Maybe he wouldn't notice her, now that he was so otherwise occupied. "It wasn't worth much, anyway." She touched the cold metal of the door, ran her fingers across its teeny grooves, not daring to take her eyes off the man who might as well have tried to kill her. He bent over his damned monitors while she groped for the door handle.

"I'll get another —" Movement caught one corner of her eye. Something moved by the body drawer that had just shocked her.

The jerk made a growling noise.

She swung her attention off of him and back onto the wall of body drawers. One of them — the one she had partially slid open, nearly getting herself killed in the process — slid out farther, as if it moved on its own. Had her motion done that?

Making it swing out by itself? Or did Brant the jerk's monitors do that? Either way, it was slowly floating out of the wall, as if an invisible hand, a *ghost* hand softly pulled it. Greer gasped. She hadn't done that.

Or had she? Maybe since she'd started to pull on its handle, the drawer opened the rest of the way. Maybe it had extra sensitive sliders, and once the motion started, it couldn't stop. Was that why he was so angry with her?

Or —

"Oh my god!" she screamed. Fingers of a human hand curled over the lip of the open drawer. Then the rest of the hand followed, and then an arm, a woman's bronzed arm, but...

Well, why not? It was a body drawer, after all. She shouldn't be surprised to see a body in it.

It's just that... She had re-thought the situation and decided the doors were actually for seagulls. Where the aliens hid.

She was wrong.

And how did the woman's arm get so tanned, having been *inside* a drawer, for god knew how long? Greer remembered back to the times she'd done the anti-aging treatments in the cryo-ward, back home in the Holland Annex, and how she'd always emerged with her youthfully regenerated skin white as a ghost.

Brant exclaimed something in what must've been the local language, since Greer didn't understand. And then the woman's head emerged from the drawer as she sat up. Her naked, mud-streaked torso followed, and Greer gasped again. God! The woman's breasts were round and full with glorious youth, not saggy at all, like those of the old hags who usually entered the drawer for anti-aging treatments.

The woman said something back, also that Greer didn't understand. Brant — typical man — stared at the woman's breasts as he rushed to her side and helped her out of the drawer. At least the woman wore something to cover up her crotch. It looked like a skirt of dangling ropes, or maybe...

Greer screamed. It was Ziza! She thought she had escaped that crazy jungle woman. What was she doing *here*? When she'd been in the jungle way up north only the night before? Trying to kill everyone and steal Molly, besides?

Now Greer wished she knew what Molly had done to turn off the machines before. If she could figure out how to do that, maybe Ziza would vanish back into her drawer. Or melt to the ground. Or...

"You can't have her!" Greer shouted. Ziza had chased them here, coming for Molly. That's why Landon had taken the little girl up the mountain to see her mother. For safekeeping! He'd known. Why hadn't he told Greer? She could've helped. Then she wouldn't be in this predicament, would she?

Greer glanced back at the monitor that had shown her Summer's image. Was Molly there with her now? Could they hear her if she screamed?

"Priiii!" Greer yelled at the top of her lungs. That was the babbling sound Molly had made when she turned off the machine. Greer didn't know what else to do. Maybe it was a cry for help. What other choice did Greer have except to cry for help?

The machines blinked and then blanked out. Their hums and clicks crackled and died. It worked! Or else, Molly had heard her cry and turned them off, even from afar.

Swishing sounds pounded outside in the corridor, and then

the metal door swung open behind Greer, bumping her away from it.

"What's going on in here?" Doctor Chan said, stepping into the laboratory.

CHAPTER TWENTY-NINE

LANDON BLINKED AND SHOOK his head, trying to shake the image of Van Pelt's blueprint receiver from his vision. But it was still there, towering before him in its stacks of cylinders and spheres, faintly humming, leaking enough pinpricks of light to glow softly in the dark, illuminating this section of the aliens' underground outpost, some sort of cavern that he'd fallen into.

Gooseflesh on the back of his neck warned him that this was no underground cavern. Not natural, that is. The floor he teetered on sucked at his feet and felt too smooth beneath his hiking boots to have formed in a natural manner.

He'd only assumed it was a cavern on account of the darkness, and underground because of his fall. But now he realized that what he'd perceived as a fall had merely been some sort of entrance. Perhaps he'd already passed through El Pastor's door, the secret gate to admit him here.

To wherever, whatever this place was.

A buffer of darkness surrounded the machine's flickers and kept him from seeing the walls of this room. He presumed it was a room that held him. Or maybe a vessel. But here in the center of the dark room, the phosphorescent glow threw out a web-like pattern on the far side of the machine. It looked as if a transparent wall stood between the machine and whatever lay beyond in the darkness.

So this was why H.F. had wanted Landon to come here to Patagonia. H.F. had known he would recognize the machine. Because it was one of the variations on Landon's own work. Van Pelt's work had been more theoretical than Landon's actual applications for instantaneous communication. Even so, they both used similar equipment, collecting and directing streams of tachyons.

H.F. had known that Van Pelt's machine would be here.

Van Pelt must have brought his machine from the Holland Annex, when he came with the team of Executors, summoned by Manrique, and then left it here. H.F. must have known about that summons and assumed the rest.

Or else H.F. had been here, too.

Landon wouldn't have known. He'd been hard at work in his own laboratory up on SpaceHab.

He shook his head and whispered, "No." Impossible. Van Pelt couldn't have brought his machine here, not unless time had distorted. Landon himself had seen the machine in Van Pelt's laboratory in the Holland Annex, and that visit had occurred *after* Van Pelt's trip here, to Patagonia.

There must be a duplicate.

Or else time *had* distorted. Somehow.

Maybe H.F. was a time traveler. Landon snorted. The old man would've loved to hear him consider that.

Yet...

More likely, Landon had seen the prototype in the Holland Annex, and this one, here in Patagonia...

This one was the actual working machine. He could tell, because of the way light spilled out, around buttons and levers.

The inner mechanisms were working now.

The glowing web pulsed as if it pressed against the perimeter of darkness.

Yes, it was working.

Why?

Had Van Pelt brought it here as part of his experiments, so that he could return to the Holland Annex and send tachyonic blueprints to this distance, several degrees of latitude away? Had his experimental blueprints, then, traveled through a slice of Earth?

But Van Pelt's laboratory had shut down following his death.

Or had it? Some research assistants must continue to have access to the laboratory.

Maybe the machine wasn't here just for the sake of experimentation. Maybe the machine was actually receiving the Tititri. Right now. *This* very machine.

This was why the alien in Molly had brought her here. To welcome her people, incoming tachyonic blueprints.

"Molly?" Landon called into the dark. If welcoming the blueprints was her purpose, then she must still be here, somewhere. Not taken through El Pastor's gate by her captors. Not yet. "Honey, it's Dad. Where are you, baby? Everything's okay. Daddy has come for you. It's time to go home now."

But she didn't answer. The alien within her had silenced her. No one answered. Not even an echo of his own, lonely words.

His breath tightened in his throat, listening for any of her little sounds. He heard instead the squish of his own pulse. Stinging tingles numbed his arm, where he'd wrapped El Pastor's braided vines and grasses too tightly, cutting off his circulation. He shook his arm, whipping the loose end of the grass braid, tugging it, unraveling it until it flicked away and thunked against one of the cylinders holding Van Pelt's machine together.

A faint earthy smell released from the braid, something familiar and pleasant, but he couldn't quite place it at first. Pleasant, but not the disorienting bakery smells he'd perceived here at first. It was more... Floral. That was it. Like the hint of roses in the baby lotion Greer liked to use to lather up Molly.

"Molly?" he cried out again.

He strained to listen, to decipher any non-mechanical sounds above the soft hum of the blueprint receiver. Something whispered from the distance with a tang of urgency. He didn't know if his imagination was playing tricks on him or if he'd actually heard the voice of his daughter.

He'd never heard her whisper before.

He stepped back from the machine, closer to the dark, and scanned into it, willing himself to see. Where was she?

There! Just beyond the reach of the machine's glow, he made out a different shape, not geometric but amorphous. A mound of some sort, lying low to the floor. It seemed to be moving.

He commanded his body to run, to head in that direction, but his feet felt like lead weights. The floor was holding him down. Straining, he overcame the force and pushed his way closer.

"Molly!"

The lump was too large to be Molly, he realized with a sinking sensation of disappointment.

Closer, he detected the fetid smells of El Pastor, overpowering the faint florals of his daughter. The shaman was bending over someone, another bundle.

"Where is she?" he said, his voice lashing out. "You're trying to hide her from me, but it won't work."

The mounds rustled and shifted. El Pastor turned to look up. "You want to say goodbye? There is still time."

"L-landon? Is that you?" The woman's voice sounded confused, but clear enough to him.

"Summer!" He pushed past the old man and knelt down beside the other lump on the floor. His ex-wife. "What has he done to you?"

She did not respond, and he whipped back to El Pastor. "What have you done to her?"

"Nothing that she did not wish for herself," said the goatherder. "She already chose her end before you arrived. I only showed her which of my herbs and roots would do the job for her."

"Her *end?*" His voice shook as it rose. "Are you saying she *poisoned* herself? And you helped her?"

"It is as she wished."

It was a waste to argue with him, and so Landon bent back over Summer. "Chan will have an antidote. Let's get you out of here. Can you stand?"

"What are you...doing here? Go away."

"Not without you." Or Molly. He wasn't leaving before he found Molly. Even if it meant not getting Summer to Chan in time. He could not fail his daughter as he'd failed his wife.

"You're...only in the way."

"Molly's here somewhere. Do you know where?"

"Mol...ilia," Summer said, her voice stalling as if with a great weight. Fear? "I thought...I thought she was *dead*. All along, they lied. Don't...don't let them..."

"I won't. But you have to tell me how to stop them from controlling her. I can't help if I don't know how."

"You must..." Her voice dropped to a whisper, but there was no one to overhear. "Take her away from here."

"That's what I'm trying to do. But you have to tell me how to stop them."

"Away..."

He wanted to shake her with his frustration. "You know, don't you? You know!"

"They lied. My whole life, everything...a lie."

"Help me help her! We have to help our daughter."

Soft, skittering sounds tapped or echoed somewhere in the distance, bouncing off a surface perhaps beyond the web of phosphorescence cast out by Van Pelt's machine. "Priiii." It was his daughter's babbling baby voice. But he could not see her.

"Molly!" He sprang away from Summer and flung himself toward the baby's sounds. He crashed against some unseen barrier. Sparks flew out from the machine, like a disturbed nest of birds. And then her babbles came from another direction, and he turned to follow those new sound streams. He whirled around, thrashing in the dark. "Where are you?"

"They want her," Summer said.

They... Tititri? "No," he said with a growl, spinning in circles, honing in on her baby gurgles. "I won't let them. They can't have her." He squinted into the dark, willing himself to interpret meaning to the shifting shapes of shadows that flitted around the periphery of Van Pelt's glowing humming machine.

"Run, baby!" Summer cried.

"Stay there, Molly," Landon said. "Daddy's coming for you."

"It's too late..." Summer coughed. "They have your tach... com."

"Who? The Tititri?" He teetered on the balls of his feet, unsure which way to lunge next. "They have my *tachcom*?" No. She was making no sense. The Tititri didn't have it, *couldn't* have it.

It was his invention, and he knew exactly where it was: already installed in the *Centaurus*, the spaceship docked at the Orbiting Launch Platform, awaiting their journey to Proxima Centauri. That's where it was. The aliens didn't have it.

She was confused, that's all.

"What you see here," he said, waving his arm in a circle, indicating this alien outpost, "is Van Pelt's doing. Not mine." Seeing Van Pelt's blueprint receiver, glowing and humming and casting a net of tachyonic blueprints, it was no wonder she was confused. Van Pelt had come the closest to replicating Landon's work, but now he wondered if his colleague might have surpassed Landon's work.

"Van Pelt," Landon continued to explain, feeling an almost irrational need to make Summer understand, "must've been working with the Tititri."

"No... The Xyvors will kill us all."

"The Savers are done." His voice lowered to a soothing level, trying to erase her frenzy as if she were a hysterical child. "They're in prison." Or dead.

"Not Savers," Summer said. "*Xyvors.*"

"Right, that's what I said." They were *her* buddies. They'd gotten her — and him — into this mess. They'd apparently turned traitor on her. "Don't worry. You're safe now with us. We'll get you back where you belong, and then the prison will keep you safe. Chan will know how to treat you for whatever you took. She'll make you well. Let's get out of here. This man knows the way out." He turned to El Pastor. "Which way?"

"No," Summer said, her voice wheezing. He wondered what herbs El Pastor had let her have. "No one is safe." She choked on a sob. "Only way out...is death..."

With Summer's laboring gasp, the baby answered from the dark with a cry. "Maaaa...miiii!"

From far away sounded a drumroll of rumbles. Thunder. Thunder?

The distant, muted roar gathered in strength and culminated with a long, drawn-out, whistling screech. A blast.

Then the underground cavern shook around them. The machines flickered and sparked. Their humming, clicking, throbbing sounds died as the pulsing web of phosphorescence flatlined. Landon felt the bones in his body vibrate as the room shifted around them.

"Noooo!" Summer thrashed on the floor, scooping up El Pastor's braid of grass and wrapping it about her. "Diamond! I thought you were my friend. I thought you meant to help me. But no. You're one of *them*."

A chill slid down Landon's neck as she called out as if someone else was here with them. He tried to move toward her, but the floor tilted, flinging him farther away. El Pastor clutched at his arm. "We must hurry to tunnel. Before it closes."

"Let's go, Summer. Give me your hand." Landon held out his hand to her, but she collapsed into a heap on the floor, the ball of her limp shape rolling back and forth.

"She wish to stay here," El Pastor said. "She want to pass so that they no control her. The grasses they will help her pass."

Landon flung him off and fell next to Summer. "No. You can't. Think of Molly."

"Mo...lilia," she whispered, her body shuddering. "Gone..." One last sigh, and life passed from her.

He shook her, trying to shake life back into her. "No! Don't leave me. Don't...die." His words broke off into violent, quavering sobs. She couldn't die. Not when... He loved her. *Always* loved her. Why hadn't she understood? Now it was too late.

From the darkness came a swishing sound, as if someone watching them had shifted position, causing garments to rustle. "Lannndon," said a woman's whispery soft voice. "Hurry."

The hairs stood on the back of his neck as he recognized the alien's voice. He looked up from Summer's body. There stood their two-year-old daughter within her own halo of radiance. Apparently, the alien within her wanted to help them escape.

CHAPTER THIRTY

GREER STUMBLED AND YELPED when the door threw her to one side, shooting a bruising pain up her arm. "Hey, watch what you're doing, would you?"

But Doctor Chan didn't pay any attention to Greer. Chan glided into the room, swishing atop the steel blades where normal people had feet.

That was just the thing. No one was normal in this prison.

"You were supposed to protect my equipment," Chan said, charging over to Brant.

A new thought crossed Greer's mind. What if she ended up *stuck* here in this monkey farm at the bottom of the Earth?

With that jungle woman — Ziza — who'd somehow followed her. Through a *drawer*.

"How'd *she* get here?" Greer blurted out, reminding the others of her presence.

But they still ignored her. As if she was invisible.

Hell.

Two guards, with weapons drawn, swept into the room behind Chan. Greer changed her mind about persisting too loudly.

"Why did you let her use the wormhole?" Chan said to Brant, sounding pissed off.

"I didn't." Brant's gaze flickered toward Greer, as if he'd

suddenly remembered she was here.

"Me?" Greer said. "You thought it was *me*? I didn't do it." She wouldn't know a wormhole from an asshole. But she bet her brother would. Just wait until she told Landon! So *that's* what was inside those drawers. A wormhole.

Brant's interest slipped off Greer as fast as it had flitted across her.

A shiver of dread seeped through Greer as she realized the more important take-away point, far more important than any silly wormhole. Ziza hadn't followed Greer. It was *Molly* that the jungle woman was still after. And somehow the wormhole in the drawer had brought her here.

Okay, Greer confessed that she might not be so smart, but she wasn't stupid, either. She could figure out that if there was one wormhole in a drawer, there would be others. And that meant that no matter where on Earth she went, Ziza would follow.

Shit.

"It's about time you showed up," Brant said to the guards. "Restrain her." He pointed at Ziza.

At least he hadn't pointed at Greer. In fact, everyone here seemed oblivious of Greer's presence. *That* didn't set well with her.

The guards closed in on Ziza.

Was Greer supposed to feel relieved? She didn't, thank you very much. She was still stuck in this god-awful place, she'd lost Molly, and now she'd found out that there was no escape from the crazy jungle woman.

But at least the guards, who were actually kind of cute, were yanking Ziza's arms around to her back and snapping cuffs in place around her wrists.

"Take her to cell block four," Brant said.

Ziza shot Greer the evil eye as the guards shoved her out of the laboratory. They passed through the door and turned right down the hall leading deeper into the prison.

Brant strode out, turning left. The exit, where Molly had cooed at her seagull through the glass doors, lay in that direction.

"Wait," Chan said, catching his sleeve. "Where do you think you're going?"

"To do my job, which is no concern of yours. I have my orders. Yours are to get the sister out of here. Keep her in sight at all times."

Was that supposed to make Greer feel better? It didn't.

Chan apparently didn't like it either, from the sound of her retort. "I don't take orders from you."

"Maybe if you did, none of this would've happened. Now I have to fix your mess." Brant broke free of Chan's grip and then rushed away, toward the building's exit.

"Mess?" Greer said. "What mess? Does he mean the jungle woman? Then, why isn't he going with the guards to lock her up? Where's he going instead?"

Chan ignored her and pulled a pad from the pocket of her lab coat. It flashed, already awake. Chan frowned at its flashing message while footsteps faded away, gates rattled and slammed, echoing in the distance. Now it was just the two of them left alone in the laboratory with god knew what else would pop out of the wormhole drawers.

"Let's go," Chan said, re-pocketing her pad. "We have to stop him."

"Why? What's he planning to do?"

"Subvert everything I've ever worked for. We'd better hurry. The director general is waiting for us in a hovercraft. You might as well come along."

"Is this another tour?"

"Yes. You can think of it as such. But try not to interfere this time, okay? Our lives could depend on it."

If she put it that way, then. Greer shivered and nodded.

* * * * *

"She chose to die," said El Pastor's gentle voice, breaking through the fog of grief that pinned Landon down. "To protect *bebé*." Landon felt a tug on his sleeve as the old man dragged him upright with surprising strength. "We must hurry now."

Landon let the shaman pull him away from Summer's body and nudge him into the dark of the subterranean cavern. He had to trust someone if he and Molly were to escape this place, this alien outpost, outfitted by Van Pelt.

"Lannnnndon," said the alien who called herself Titinha and used Molly as her speaking platform. "This way."

It pained him to leave Summer's body behind, but right now he had to consider Molly's safety. He didn't want this place to become their tomb as well.

Molly stood, her small figure spotlighted in a faint pool of luminescence. The machines that ensnared alien tachyons gave off a glowing light and caught his daughter's eyes. Sparkling green, her eyes focused on Landon's approach.

"My people are safe here," the alien said through Molly, "as blueprints."

"The place is collapsing," Landon said. "How is that safe?"

"Not exactly. PRI is adjusting the position of the probe to ensure its safety. You might feel some shifting, but the floor will absorb most of the sensation. Still, you must step carefully. And once you return to your people, you must guard the secret of my people's presence."

"Why should I? First, you took my wife. Now my daughter."

"You will have her back. Your daughter will be released once the transference is complete."

"What transference? When? What about my *wife*?"

"I am sorry. She was a mistake. She was merely the carrier of your daughter who was created for the purpose of hosting the Titinha. Your daughter is not a permanent host. The Titinha promises you that."

"What good is your promise? You already screwed up. She was my *wife!*"

"The Titinha is the leader of the Tititri, and as such, has the power to honor a promise, unlike the rebel faction of our people. They have lost faith in our future because of the Xyvor invaders who have set our world of Ti onto a path of doom."

"Invaders?" H.F.'s alien invaders. Except, this alien outpost wasn't for the purpose of bringing dormant invaders to Earth, as H.F. had thought. Instead, it held blueprints of alien refugees, fleeing from invaders.

"We must await the time when this body grows enough to become sufficiently dexterous. Then your daughter will return here to activate the transference of my people to the new bodies your doctor will have built for us. Meanwhile, you must finish the job that has brought us this far."

Molly turned from her spotlight and skipped into the dark.

"Wait!" Landon called.

Someone nudged him from behind — El Pastor — and Landon stumbled. He fought for his balance to stay upright and lumbered, feeling awkward under the burden of shock that gripped him with Summer's so unnecessary death.

Not to mention the aliens.

Now the alien was using Molly's tiny body to lead him out of this place. So that he could finish a job. It all seemed...so impossible.

"Wait!" he called again into the dark. "Finish what job?"

"Find the alignment in time," Molly whispered, or the alien inside Molly whispered, but in any case, his daughter's body skipped onward into the dark, and Landon fought to keep her in sight.

It wasn't easy in the semi-dark, but his daughter glowed, as if her little body had absorbed the phosphorescent light thrown off by the alien-capturing machines in this alien receptacle under the glacier. From the distance, which only seemed to grow between them, she looked like a flickering candle disappearing ahead. She moved swiftly, with too much self-assurance and knowledge for a two-year-old.

And then suddenly she stopped before a spinning, tumbling wall of ice.

Landon stumbled, torn between following an alien, losing his daughter, and not wanting to leave Summer. He caught up to Molly on some sort of threshold, waiting, and finally a hole cracked open in the wall of ice.

"Go," said El Pastor, pushing him from behind.

* * * * *

Greer felt like a chastised teenager, strapped into her seat in the hovercraft between Doctor Chan and Director General Raimundo Manrique. As if those two thought they were her chaperones, and sitting between the two of them would keep her from acting out. Not that *that* would stop her, if she so chose.

What *did* stop her was terror.

Not terror from her chaperones, no.

It was the mountains.

Peaks filled the window bubble overhead like giant shadows, and their nearness sent chills down the back of her neck. The hovercraft skimmed so close that their passage stirred grit from the side of the mountains, and chunks of dirt and pebbles rattled back against the craft. At least that's what she hoped it was. At any moment, she felt sure, they would crash.

Greer sat frozen, her fingers wrapped tightly around her seat strap. Her gaze fixed to the back of the pilot's head, sending him mental messages to stay alert. He must've taken the craft off autopilot, thinking he would give the passengers some sort of cheap thrill ride. Her chaperones on either side of her babbled away, completely unaware. Didn't they care that they were about to crash and die? If Greer managed to survive the night, she was gonna kill Landie for sure for bringing her down here to the bottom of nowhere.

It slowly dawned on her what her chaperones were talking about.

"He wants to capture the little girl," Chan was saying. "And I'm the one who sent them out there."

"Do not blame yourself," Raimundo said. "You could not have known."

"But I did know. I saw the variation when I read her chip. The child is not...human. I wanted to know what she would do, if confronted by the equipment, so I left the lab open for her to find."

"And what did she do?"

"There's something out there, in the artifact, that she can communicate with."

"Molly?" Greer blurted out. "What have you done to Molly?"

Chan went on, as if Greer hadn't spoken. "And now he's going to ruin everything. He was supposed to oversee security in my lab, not sabotage the project. And we're so close. The inmates have almost completed the road. Another day or two, and I could've started transporting the equipment back to our labs."

"Perhaps it would be better to leave them buried under the ice," Raimundo said. "We can't be sure of their intentions."

"A little ice won't stop them."

"Stop *who*?" Greer's fingers released from her straps and balled into fists. "Ziza?" Ziza wanted Molly, god knew why. "She's already locked up. She is, isn't she? Or does she have some pals you're worried about?" The aliens. Oh god.

If looks could kill, then Greer was dead from the chilling glance that Chan sent her way.

"You know about them," Greer said, not to be put off. "Don't you?"

It wasn't *her* fault that Landon's super duper classified secret was out. He couldn't blame her for letting it slip out. These two already knew about the aliens. Heck, they were *experimenting* on aliens. Ziza must be one of them. That's why she'd popped out of one of Chan's drawers. And not only that,

Chan was planning to dig up more of them from the ice and haul them down the mountain.

And Brant the jerk was trying to grab Molly for Chan, who probably wanted to stuff the baby into one of her drawers. Do some horrible experiments on her. All because of the green-eyed woman who sometimes appeared on Molly's face.

Greer wouldn't let them, not if it took the last breath in her body.

"We knew that someone was intent on destroying the artifact," Chan said. "We did not expect it to be our own warden."

"Perhaps," Raimundo said, "he is not actually the warden sent by the Executors but an infiltrator instead."

"What matters now," Chan said, turning to Greer, "is that your brother and niece have inserted themselves in the way. They will become collateral damage if we do not hurry."

Greer shivered, not sure which threat was greater. Death, or capture.

* * * * *

Landon lunged through the hole that opened up in the wall of ice. Following Molly, he entered the icy cold of a tunnel, scarcely wider than Landon's body. El Pastor stumbled behind him, and the hole in the ice closed up. The cavernous room with machines disappeared from sight, hidden behind a shifting wall of ice.

Wind slid along the sides of the tunnel and smacked him, pushing him back, rattling the fabric of his coat. Yet, Molly danced onward, seemingly unaffected by the wind resistance. Walls of ice lined the tunnel and glittered, reflecting Molly's passage through the ice. Somehow, she had known exactly where to find this passage.

It wasn't Molly. It was an alien leading the way. The alien wanted him out of there, so that he could "finish" the job. His work with tachyons apparently had something to do with an alignment. He would find it, he suspected, on the mission to Proxima Centauri. That's why he had to go. And he had to keep the alien presence secret.

Or else, what? Or else the alien wouldn't ever release Molly?

He wasn't sure he should test the alien to find out. He wasn't sure of a lot of things.

For instance, leaving Summer's body behind. He did not like doing that, but he couldn't carry the body if he had to keep up with Molly.

He pressed on, through the tunnel of ice.

He had not gotten his answers from Summer. Now her death would keep him from ever finding out what her fragile mind had known. As Van Pelt's death had also kept the alien secret safe.

He understood, or so he thought: Van Pelt and Summer had chosen to die instead of allowing the aliens to control them.

Not Landon. He would not die, at least not as they had. He would never give up until he freed Molly. He sprinted after her.

* * * * *

Searchlights flashed from the belly of the hovercraft. A puddle of light dropped into the night, flooding the glacier below. Chan and Raimundo leaned closer to the windows, peering at the eerie, sparkling reflection of silvery ice. Greer looked, too.

There he was. The jerk. She'd recognize his tall, skinny frame anywhere, the way he strode around as if a rod stuck through you-know-where. But there was someone else she didn't recognize, someone wearing an orange jumpsuit. Oh yeah, the orange jumped out in the blazing lights from the hovercraft.

The two men down there ducked and cringed, as if they thought the hovercraft was about to land on top of them. And heck, maybe that was Chan's plan all along. Not that she could blame her for such a plan.

Then the guy in the orange suit aimed something at them. Long and pointed. A rifle, oh god oh god!

The pilot saw it too and punched some buttons that made the hovercraft lurch, out of the line of fire. The lights from the craft instantly switched off, and night swallowed them.

Raimundo swore. "It's the one they call Diamond. The Assassin. Where'd he get the weapon?"

Greer closed her eyes. She couldn't watch the end happening around her.

Chan kept yakking. "Brant must've arranged it for him. We've got to get down there. Now."

"No ma'am," the pilot said, just as firm.

The craft jerked from side to side. Greer muttered a prayer, the first time in years.

"Too dangerous." How did the pilot manage to remain so unruffled? "That prisoner is holding one of our officers hostage."

Greer's eyes popped open. "No he isn't. More likely, they've got Molly!"

"We've got to stop them," Chan said. "He wasn't supposed to let anyone get hurt."

"Molly!" Greer screamed, as if anyone down there could hear her. "He's after Molly! And Landie!"

Something flared from the glacier below and zipped through the night, angling towards the hovercraft. A fireball the size of a nugget, it hit the side of the craft with another burst of sparks. They rocked backwards and dropped. Greer strained against her seat straps and fought the sick taste of bile, along with her whole stomach, rising in her throat.

"Hang on tight," said the pilot, completely unfazed, gripping his control stick.

Heaviness suddenly crashed down on her head, and with one more yank, the craft stabilized. Her heart fluttered, and she breathed again.

Just in time. A booming sound split the air, and the craft shuddered, bumping in the wake of the disturbance.

"What is it?" Raimundo said. "Did they do that?"

"No sir," the pilot said. "Avalanche." He switched on lights, flooding the mountain.

Greer thought for a minute that her vision went double, and then she realized it was the mountain shaking beneath them. The field of ice shifted, as if the mountain shrugged off its coat of ice. Chunks of ice rolled and tumbled and roared. The two men down there looked like rag dolls flopping around as the side of the mountain heaved. An island of ice separated from the glacier and hurled the men over the side of a precipice.

"No!" Greer sobbed and clawed at her seat straps. "Landie and Molly are down there, too! We've got to save them!"

Chan rested a cold hand on Greer's arm. "It's too late."

"Maybe not." Raimundo pointed at a gaping hole, exposed in the aftermath of the passage of ice.

* * * * *

A pinprick of light switched on in the distance ahead, flashing like a searchlight, signaling, Landon hoped, the end of the tunnel. Suddenly Molly stopped, as if frozen by headlights. She turned and waited for Landon to catch up. He caught her in his arms and lifted her up, cradling her to his chest.

"Daaaa." Molly leaned her head against him. Her eyes had lost the alien green.

"My baby," he said, crooning and nuzzling her. The alien was gone, for now.

The searchlight bounced, and a distant man's voice hollered down at them through the ice tunnel. "Doctor Walker? Are you in there?"

"Here," Landon said.

With Molly in his arms and El Pastor on his heels, Landon emerged from the tunnel to find Director General Manrique waving the searchlight. It was the dark of night, but it was also open air, where glacier coated a basin punched into the side of the mountain. The thrum of a waiting hovercraft pounded the air, stirring ice crystals in Landon's face. He sucked in a lungful of open air.

"Thank goodness," Manrique said. "We found you."

Greer pushed past Manrique and flung herself sobbing against Landon. She wrapped her arms around him and Molly. "Oh, Landon! Thank god! It was horrible! Just horrible!"

"Calm down, Greer."

"It was a... There was a..." Greer hiccuped on her words before spitting the rest out. "He tried to *kill* us!"

"Who did?"

"That prisoner! He had something to blow us all up. I screamed, and that stopped him, all right, but only for a minute, and then..."

"And then what?"

Manrique interjected while Greer gasped, choking on tears. "There has been a terrible accident. A big piece of the glacier broke off and fell to the canyon far below. It took two of our people with it. I am afraid that our warden, Brant Hermanson, he is gone. And we lost another prisoner, one who calls himself 'Diamond'."

"Diamond?" Landon spit out the word. Summer had cried out to Diamond, whom she'd thought had been a friend. But he was one of *them*, she'd said. An alien?

"Because I screamed at him, Landie," Greer said. "And that's not all. Wait till you see what's in that lab —"

Manrique jabbed her and clamped one hand over her mouth. He glanced over his shoulder at the waiting hovercraft. A ramp extended onto the remains of the glacier. Through the glowing window, Chan sat beside the pilot at the controls and gave them a thumbs up.

Manrique leaned close to Landon. "We will return to my office where you can tell me what the Executors would not."

Landon shrugged. "I cannot speak for them. I have no complete answers."

Manrique shook his head and chuckled softly. "Do you expect me to believe their report, my friend?"

"The depression down there," Landon said, "probably caused the instability that led to that chunk of glacier calving."

Manrique scoffed. "Clearly, there *is* something down there.

And this tunnel we found you in, it leads to it, correct?"

"It seems to have collapsed."

Manrique scowled. "I do not believe that it is a leftover missile as the Executors claimed. It is an artifact. I expected answers from you. I must know if I am right. About the...you know what."

Aliens, that's what he meant, but apparently the director general didn't want to speak the word aloud in front of the others.

Alien outpost, H.F. had said.

Guard their secret, the alien had said through Molly.

Only then would she be released.

Molly wiggled in his arms, transferring to Greer's arms.

Transference. The alien wanted to transfer its people into new bodies.

Landon thought about his role, protecting Molly. Surviving the future. What would he tell Manrique?

"No," he finally said with a sigh. "There's no artifact. There was nothing down there."

CHAPTER THIRTY-ONE

THE MORNING SUN ROSE IN a clear sky. Wind had blown away the clouds and mist that had shrouded the peaks, unveiling their mysteries. The prison van rattled to a stop at the edge of the airstrip where the shearjet awaited.

Landon bent down to his travel bag tucked between his feet. He unlatched the bag and reached inside, pawing through the inner pocket until he touched the sleek stick of data. His fingers curled around the tiny object that contained H.F.'s message. He withdrew his fist, along with the stick, and then snapped the bag shut again.

"Are you sure you do not wish to change your mind about what happened up there last night?" Manrique nodded at the mountains.

"Oh!" Greer said, gushing as she unbuckled Molly from her seat. "It was just horrible! Those poor men. I thought for sure that chunk of glacier was going to throw all of us right over the edge —"

"Greer." Landon lowered his voice to a rumbling pitch of warning. He waggled his brows and snatched Molly from his sister's arms. They'd escaped.

"It is your last chance before you return to Goiás," Manrique said. "There is still time for you to tell me what you saw."

"I already told you." Landon backed out of the van with Molly in his arms and one fist balled. "It was a depression. Unstable ice. We're very lucky. Let's leave it at that." He knew his priorities now, better than ever. Molly. He would protect his daughter at all costs. He was the only parent she had now.

Manrique whistled through his teeth. "What will you tell Samuel?"

Landon shook his head. "If he still wants me on the mission, then Molly has to come with me. We'll put her in cryo-sleep." It was the safest choice. As long as Molly slept, so would the Titinha within her.

He waited until Manrique, Greer, and the driver turned their backs on him, preoccupied with fetching the remainder of the luggage. Then he tossed the data stick away in an overhand pitch toward the field at the edge of the airstrip.

"Birrrr…" Molly gurgled and giggled, watching the soaring angle of his toss.

"No, honey," Landon said. "No more birds. It's just you and me, from here on."

* * * * *

About the Author

Rebecca S.W. Bates writes science fiction, fantasy, and mystery under a variety of pen names. She is the author of the Centauri Series and several dozen short stories, including appearances in Fiction River's *Fantasy Adrift* and *Universe Between* and in the Colorado Book Award nominated *Broken Links, Mended Lives.* Her latest novels include *Murder with Altitude, The Mound Dwellers,* and *The Jigsaw Window*, which are available in all formats from most book retailers. *Sphinx of Centaurus*, the third novel of the Centauri Series, will be released from D.M. Kreg Publishing in late 2016. Sample first chapters and her collections of short stories at www.dmkregpublishing.com. To find out more about her works and her inspiration, visit her at rebeccawriter.blogspot.com.

The Centauri Series

The Signal #1

Prelude to Proxima #2

Sphinx of Centaurus #3 (coming in 2016)

Sharing Sol: three short stories about the challenges of space exploration when somebody else is also out there.

Other short story collections:

Tough Mothers: three stories about mothering in space

The Time Is Light: three stories about distortions in space and time

Three Goofy Stories: three stories about a wizard, a rabbit hole, and some pigs

Tightropes through the Eco: three stories about saving the environment (coming in 2016)

Read selections at www.dmkregpublishing.com

Following is an excerpt from "Titan Towers," a short story in

Sharing Sol in the world of the **Centauri Series**

from

Rebecca S.W. Bates

Available now from D.M. Kreg Publishing

Titan Towers

Walker sat dimly aware, shaking against the straps of his bucket seat, inhaling the scent of...burning ozone? Antiseptics? He blinked furiously against the white haze obscuring his vision and detected instrument panels lining the circular space that surrounded him.

He was inside the lander.

Two shadowy shapes moved about him, whispering, rocking the lander side to side. Crewmates. He had to assist whatever they were doing. Tried to move. Couldn't flex so much as a finger. The after-effects of cryogenics left him in a state of paralyzing detachment. They'd warned him about this possible side effect. Impaired vision, too. For a man who liked to control his environment and everyone within range, he might as well have died already.

No!

Understanding seeped through him, cell by cell, warming him drip by drip, like a narcotic in reverse. They hadn't planned to awaken him until orbit was achieved.

Now he was awake.

Which meant they must be there...here. Titan.

He hadn't wanted to separate from his bride for as long as this first manned mission to the surface of Saturn's famous moon would require, but the boss had insisted. No one refused

H.F. Washington.

In spite of his reluctance to play astronaut, Landon couldn't hold back the tidal forces of elation that swept through him now, trying to thaw the paralysis of his mind.

A billion plus kilometers, and Landon had slept through the entire journey.

"Dr. Walker?" said a honeyed voice, as sweet as Summer's. Couldn't be his wife's. Summer opted to live with her parents in Colorado during his absence.

"Dr. Walker?" said the woman's voice again, not Summer's. "How do you feel?"

A face bent over his face, flooding his hazed vision. Her smell of antiseptics washed over him. He couldn't remember her name.

"Just nod if you hear me," she said. "How do you feel?"

Never better, he meant to say with intended sarcasm, but the words didn't emerge, either.

"It's okay, don't try to speak," she said. "I should let you know that we have a slight problem."

"Pro'lem?" He managed to spit out the dreaded word, the word no one wanted to hear in unforgiving space.

"Shhhh," she said, patting his hand. Her touch felt hot on his flesh. Giselle. That was her name. "We're going to have to speed things up, that's all, transferring into the float-rover. The lander put us down slightly off course. Instead of landing on one of the islands, as we expected, we landed in the middle of an ethane sea. We're sinking. Captain Norris is preparing for ejection. We just hoped we'd get to use the lander a bit longer than this."

Landon's lips twitched, trying to form words to the protest

that clutched his mind. H.F. had planned for such a possibility, considering the extent of Titan's ethane seas. They'd run through the drills. He tried to unbuckle. A muscle spasmed.

"Relax," Giselle said, massaging his arm beneath the seat straps. "Nothing you can do about it. I'm going to add a stimulant to your feeder to help with post-awakening. Might give you a headache for a bit. Don't worry about it. We'll help you transfer at the last possible moment. Your equipment is already on board the float-rover, so your project is not in danger."

Her words spun around in his head like a swarm of Summer's precious rescued bees. Giselle whisked away. The meaning of her words stewed inside him.

He channeled all of his mental strength into his body, sending brain commands to each of his extremities, but nothing responded. He could almost feel the ice that had frozen him for a billion kilometers shifting and breaking apart. He was going to have to wait out the thaw. He couldn't speed it up. He didn't wait well, idle.

He was aware of movement around him as his colleagues raced from instrument to instrument. They'd all known that the lander was a one-way trip. The lander wasn't supposed to get them off this moon. *That* ride would come from a cone-shaped capsule riding piggy-back atop the float-rover that the captain was preparing — without Landon's help — to eject from the lander.

The question was, how far down into the sea had the lander sunk already? After detachment, the float-rover could navigate under the sea for short depths, down to a couple hundred meters. It could probably rise to the surface, unless they started from too far down. The seas were a kilometer deep in places.

Nothing he could do about it.

Summer's bees buzzed through his mind, and he drifted. It would be all right. Got to trust H.F. His people would find a way out. Got to trust... Got to trust...

* * * * *

www.ingramcontent.com/pod-product-compliance
Lightning Source LLC
Chambersburg PA
CBHW071308250626
47159CB00004B/1349